DARKLING

K.M. Rice

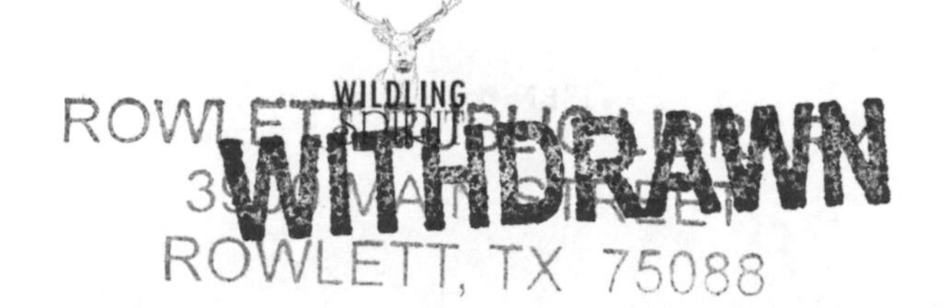

Published by Wildling Spirit
Cover art by Lindsey Crummett © 2016
Interior art by K.M. Rice © 2017
Author photo by Kassandra Thomsen Photography © 2016

ISBN: 978-1-947944-01-5

For those we have loved and lost

Chapter One

The woods are dark and my mother weaves dried blossoms into my hair. They have to be dried because there hasn't been a flower in over a year. Not since the darkness spread, veiling our valley in shadow. Which is why I am being readied for him.

I stand before my little brother Jasper who is clasping his hands and observing my mother's handiwork. He is only seven but still he knows what I am about to do. I'm wearing my mother's wedding dress. I was surprised it was such a perfect fit, for I am seventeen and she was twenty when she wed my father. It used to be white, but the lace has a tinged yellow quality from age, and there are a few holes in places where moths or mice have chewed. But it's good enough, and we aren't people who need much. Mending the holes would be too much effort when I'm only going to be in the dress for a short while.

Jasper shifts his weight, standing on his tippy toes for a moment, trying to see the top of my head. My mother has twined my blonde curls in the front, reaching behind my skull like a circlet.

I smile at Jasper. "Does it look pretty?"

Jasper nods. He is distracted by a knock on the door and moves to peer out the window. Our cabin is small, only one room, really, with some quilts hung up to separate Jasper and my sleeping area from the main room with the fireplace. The hearth glows brightly, the heart of our house, providing most of the light in the room. He used to sleep in my parents' bed but started sleeping with me after what happened to Scarlet. She is our older sister. *Was* our older sister.

Jasper lets my friend Draven in. He is dressed in a dark green tunic and leather trousers, the finest he owns. His dirty blonde curls are pulled back into a stubby ponytail, but even then, a few are escaping.

"Good morning, Draven," my mother says.

Some traditions never die. It would be just after dawn if dawn still existed. Now the only difference between night and day are the stars and moon. Though lately it has been so cloudy and cold that it is easy to lose track of the time. I haven't seen the moon in months.

"Good morning," he replies to her even though his dark brown eyes are latched onto mine. "Willow, can I speak with you?"

I nod. There isn't really anywhere we can go to find privacy so we step over to my bed.

"Willow, what you're doing... is... is honorable, but I don't think it's right."

He's the only one who knows my secret. Now I regret him knowing because the look in his eyes is making me feel guilty. His jaw is strong and dusted with brown stubble. Somewhere in-between the sun and darkness we grew up. "It has to be me," I say.

"It's not fair. Why?"

"They're here," Jasper says, peeking out of the window.

Fixing my gaze on Jasper, I try to step past Draven but he grabs my shoulder. "Why?" he repeats.

I close my eyes for a moment because I want to turn around and hug him. I want to feel his stubble on my cheek. Smell the pine and leather that stain him. Hear his heartbeat and never go out the door. But I don't turn to face him. I can't. So instead, I rest my hand over his.

"You know why," I whisper.

He pivots his hand to grab mine, to squeeze it. I wait for the words that might make me reconsider. The pledge that would admit we are more than just old friends. But they don't come and I have enough fear of my own. I don't need his cowardice added to it. So I pull my hand from his and step over to my little brother.

Jasper pulls away from the window and before the curtain falls back into place, I can glimpse their torches. The villagers have gathered at my door. It won't be long now.

Draven brushes past us all and slips outside. He is upset, and for a moment I wonder if I am making a mistake. But what I'm doing will save my family. We can't continue in such a state of deprivation. It isn't fair. And I can no longer stand by, watching the ones I love suffer when I know that there's a chance I could help. I won't say that I'm not afraid, though. I am afraid. I don't know what will happen once I am his. Maybe I won't be able to convince him to spare us.

Hair pinches my scalp as my mother tucks the last dried blossom into my locks. She holds up a mirror in front of me, showing me her handiwork. I force a smile that I don't feel. She really has done a beautiful job. The pale pink, purple and yellow pea blossoms enhance the gold of my curls. Though I am smiling, I catch my pair of green eyes staring back at me, sullen in my pale face. I blink, realizing that I'll have to make my eyes smile, as well as my lips, if I'm ever going to convince my family that this is what I want.

"It's beautiful," I say then hug my mother.

The door opens and my father steps in. He is wearing his cleanest trousers and waistcoat and pulls off his knitted cap as he enters. He fidgets with it for a moment as he looks me over, a sad smile forming on his lips. "Didn't think I'd be giving you away so soon."

Though I try as hard as I can to make my smile look real, I know it is tinged with sadness. Not the same sadness as his, but a different kind. I know he's remembering Scarlet and thinking of me as a little girl Jasper's age. Instead, I'm thinking of me as a woman my mother's age, about to give her all for her family. His blue eyes are beginning to shimmer in the firelight and I feel my throat tighten in response so I look away. Now is not the time for weakness. Now is the time to hold my head up.

I have a plan. At five foot five, I am not the tallest girl in our village, Morrot. My curves often attract attention, for I can't hide my cleavage in a dress, but I am not the prettiest girl in our village. Not the smartest, either. That was my sister, Scarlet. The one thing I am is a good listener.

People come to me with their problems. Strangers confide secrets that they have no business sharing. They each need help. They are drawn to me with instant trust. Which is why I'm the only one in the village who has the potential to make him happy. I haven't told any of this to anyone. If I did, my family would try to stop me. So I keep quiet, as I always have. I don't share secrets.

Looking at the faces of those I love, I stand up straighter. The drums begin outside. I hold my hand out and Jasper takes it. I look back to my father and he nods. Jasper leads me to the door but my mother stops me.

"Willow, wait." She grabs a white veil off of the table. It is made of an expensive, shimmering fabric, like spider's webs, and was a gift from my father on her wedding day. Attached to an ivory comb, it might be the most expensive thing we have in the house. A trinket from a time long past. My mother gently sticks the comb into the back of my head. I feel the veil lightly brush my bare shoulders. "There."

I smile at my mother, forcing the expression into my eyes. "Thank you."

She kisses my cheek, holding my chin in her hands for several long moments while her blue gaze searches mine. "You have your grandmother's eyes."

I've been told that ever since I can remember. Grandma Abella with the clear, sea-green eyes. Grandma Abella who always knew more than she should and argued with people who weren't there. Grandma Abella who wandered off muttering to herself and was found dead days later. We are more alike than even my mother knows, for Grandma Abella was good at listening, too. Maybe too good. Keeping so many secrets drove her mad.

The drums are growing louder now so I pull my chin out of my mother's calloused fingers. I nod to Jasper who tugs on the lever, opening the door. I am met with the darkness of our days, illuminated by torches and distant bonfires in the hills surrounding our village. With the trees dying, fuel will one day be scarce, but today is exceptional. The drumming is louder outside but I can't see the drummers. The thumping is primal and scared, like my heart.

The villagers form two columns, illuminating the pathway between them with their torches raised high enough for me to pass through. I squeeze Jasper's hand. Once I walk through the glowing tunnel, there is no turning back. Our traditions forbid it. I cannot falter now.

So I take my first step over the threshold, away from the light of our hearth. Then another. Jasper leads me, his hand so small in mine. If I look to my left or to my right, I will be able to name every person that I pass. But I don't. Because I can't fake a smile for all of these people. Only my family gets that much effort.

Yet still I see Bram the miller and his daughter, Megan, one of my friends. Her red hair glows in the orange light, her face gaunt. The drums beat with my every step, like the pulse of the village. When I recognize Draven's ponytail and see the quivering of his jaw, I force myself to stare straight ahead.

At last I reach the end of the glowing tunnel and find a carriage waiting for me. Not a carriage, really, but a hay wagon that hasn't been used in a year since there is no more hay. It has been adorned with pine boughs. I can't imagine where they found the greenery, since no one dares enter the woods anymore. That's where the darkness began.

No one really knows why the light dimmed. It started about five years ago, when I was twelve. Hunters noticed shadows in the forest. Shadows that grew and spread as time passed. It had always been dim beneath the boughs, but now to venture into the forest means to walk into blackest night. The hunters can no longer see to aim their arrows. Our crops are dead. Our cows dried up then died. We are starving.

Midsummer used to be a day of feasts and dances and bonfires. A day when cares were set aside for the joy of grass between our toes, warm hands in our palms, laughter in our hearts. Our celebrations dimmed with the light. Our ancestors said our bonfires asked the sun to keep burning beyond the solstice. But something has upset the balance of our woods. Something so deep that even our bonfires can't lure the sun back. And he has something to do with it. Of that we're sure now, which is why I'm being given to him.

Today is Midsummer, I remind myself, staring at the wagon that will bear me to my fate. Jasper climbs onto the bed, having trouble getting in because of his short legs. He is small for his age because he hasn't been fed properly his whole life. I take my seat beside him, careful not to snag my mother's wedding dress on the coarse wood. Several men pull the cart. The last horse in our village died three months ago.

The people of Morrot follow, their torches forming a glowworm behind the wagon. They begin to sing Midsummer's Song low and slow. I remember it being sung fast when I was a child, dancing around the bonfires, my skin golden from the sun. Now it is so pale that it nearly glows in the darkness and the song is a dirge.

"Behold the joy of children
Behold the joy of men,
Behold the burning circle
That never has an end.

Through falling leaves and winter snow
The sun will visit those below
And warm the Netherworld will be
But it's not there that you'll find me.

Behold the joy of children

Behold the joy of men,
Behold the burning circle
That never has an end.

Through spring meadows and summer sky,
The sun will shine on you and I
For we are young and dance around
Bonfires shining above ground."

The chorus is repeated as the cart rattles on. I revel in the scent of the boughs adorning the wagon. I had almost forgotten what pine sap smells like.

"Why can't I come see you?" Jasper asks in a whisper.

"Because it's your job to take care of mother and father now. You know they'll be sad without me at home."

"I'll be sad, too."

I wrap an arm around his thin shoulders, hugging him to me. I don't tell him that I am already sad. That at the sight of his pain, if I could take all this back, I would. But it's too late. I've gone through the glowing tunnel. To turn back now would not only insult our village elder, who approved of me, but also bring such shame upon my family that we would become outcasts. Food is already hard enough to come by as a community. I could never let my loved ones be cast out to fend for themselves, no matter how much time I want to spend with my little brother.

The wagon stops so far from the village that the bonfires on the hills are now mere specks of light. They look like they're floating in the dark. Like golden stars.

"Whether in this life or the next,
Even after sunset in the west
The light will return from high above..."

I lean in to Jasper's ear. My throat is tight and my vision blurring with tears. Tears that I won't let fall as I whisper the end of the song in his ear.

"For it is my heart and you are my love."

"Hail!" the villagers yell as one as they finish their song.

Elias, our village elder, stands upon a stump, bearing a torch. The drums continue and Elias holds out a withered hand, his long nails curving at the tips of his fingers. I kiss Jasper's cheek then slide off the wagon. Elias has been our leader my whole life.

I can feel the heat from Elias' torch as I approach. I can't tell how old he is, but his lithe form is still limber and spry. His pale blue eyes shimmer in the light as he looks down at me, his red lips wet, as if he's been licking them. But his gaze is somewhere below my eyes, like he is looking at my chest.

"Welcome," he shouts, flinging his arms out and addressing the crowd. "To this most glorious occasion."

The villagers ring the stump, their torches casting such strange shadows on their faces that I can no longer tell who is who, which is just as well. I'm not good at goodbyes. I look back for Jasper but can't find him. Elias continues leading the ceremony while my eyes frantically dart about, hunting for my little brother. I have no idea what Elias is saying because my heart is now hammering so loud that it's nearly drowning out the drums and I can't find Jasper. Then I spot him, off to the side, my father's large hands resting on his shoulders. I can't go to him. I just needed to see his face once more.

Elias has finished, I realize, for he steps off the stump and bows to me. The drums pause as the rest of the villagers bow, as well. In the quiet, all I hear are distant whispers. I am tempted to steal another look at my family but know that it will only make it worse if I do. They are no longer my family.

I belong to him. And it is time.

I hold my head high and gather my mother's wedding dress, lifting the front enough to walk. I tug the veil out my hair and set it down on the stump. It's worth too much to take with me and my family will need whatever they can get their hands on to trade.With a deep breath, I turn my back on Morrot. My home. My brother. Draven. The drums begin as soon as I turn, slow and heavy. Facing the woods, I can only see the trunks of the trees and smell the scent of musky earth and rotting leaves. The drums pulse louder, urging me onwards, so I take my first step into the darkness.

I am the sacrifice.

Chapter Two

The drums pulse in the distance. I don't know what will happen once they stop. My mother's wedding dress rustles as it drags along the forest floor. Lace adorns the sleeves that aren't really sleeves, just straps across my biceps. Off the shoulder, I think she called it. In the dim light of the torches, I can see that the hem is already browning with dead leaves and small pinecones clinging to the lace. A train adorned by the trees, as if they're also urging me onwards with the drums.

Sacrifice Rock is in the clearing ahead, though I can hardly see it outside of the light of the torches. It's just a vaguely grey blob out of the corners of my eyes when I turn my head. We discovered long ago that in dim light, we have better vision from the sides of our eyes than looking straight at something. Probably to detect predators attacking from our flanks. Predators. My heart feels like a rabbit's.

The drums are hammering behind me as I approach Sacrifice Rock. It is the size of a large table and slanted, leaning into the forest floor at an angle. From what I can make out, vines cling and curve around its surface. I briefly wonder how they have survived when I am distracted by a dark stain in the middle. Blood.

In the beginning, we laid out a share of our meager crops, hoping to appease the Bringer of Darkness, even though we weren't sure who or what that was. Nothing changed. Realizing we'd have to give more, each villager was assessed. My friend Draven had the largest remaining flock of chickens, so one was selected and sacrificed on the rock. When still nothing changed, we tried a sheep then a cow and despite worry over wasting whole carcasses, a pig. All the offerings were slaughtered and left at Sacrifice Rock. But no matter what the Bringer took, he wanted more, and the darkness continued to spread.

Parties were sent to seek help outside of our mountain valley but never returned. The steep slopes are dangerous in the dark and if the men didn't fall to their deaths, they froze. Without the sun, glaciers have grown in the mountain passes and we're trapped.

There is nothing left for us to try but a live human offering.

A roar rises in the distance. The villagers have cried out in unison with the final bang of the drum. I was meant to be on the rock by then. Running the few feet left, I hurl myself onto its chilly surface.

For a moment I think I can still hear the drum, ands then I realize it's my own heart pounding in my ears. I am panting, not daring to move off of the stone as if, somehow, it will keep me from drowning. My pale arms glow almost as much as my mother's dress in the shadows. I do my best to quiet my breathing and listen.

He will come. I am his.

Lying down with my back on the rock, I close my eyes and try to relax my mind. My soft belly makes me feel far too easy to shred. Cold creeps across my skin and for the first time since leaving the house, I realize that I'm chilled. I've been forced to grow used to the cold, yet even so, lying against stone, I wish I was wearing more. Opening my eyes, I wait for them to adjust to the shadows. I used to think it was impossible to see on a moonless night but after five years, my eyes have changed. Now I wonder if it would be hard to see in the sunlight.

I have no means to measure time. The drums stopped long ago, that much I know. The only sounds around me are the dripping of the trees. As I lie and wait, my body relaxes and I almost feel comfortable, as if I wasn't waiting for my potential death. Then again, we're all waiting for our deaths from the moment we're born.

It's nearly noon. It must be. My dress is damp from the dew and my joints are stiff so I know I've been here for hours. A spark of irritation warms me and for a moment I'm amused by my annoyance that my killer isn't on time. Then again, I don't believe he really is a killer, which is why I volunteered. He is troubled. I will listen to his secrets and help him, just as I have always done for friends and strangers. That's how I'll spare my family.

My mind is snapped back into my body by a noise. Something near me shifts and I hold my breath. That was no drop of water or falling branch. That was something on the forest floor. Like a foot. And it was inches away from my head.

A new cold slithers up my spine, tingling behind my ears. All this time I have been waiting for the Bringer to come when I needn't have. He was already here. Watching me.

My heart is picking up again and I try to breathe deeply to slow it down. There's another shift then an exhale on my skin. A cold finger rests on my collarbone, sending a jolt through me.

Instinct takes over and it's all I can do to keep from pulling away.

"Please," I whisper.

All I can see above me is a vaguely darker shadow. Can he feel me shaking?

I wait for cold steel in my belly, wanton hands on my flesh, claws on my skin, anything. The finger slides down my collarbone and falls off my shoulder, as if tugged by gravity. The shadow pivots and his footsteps retreat.

I sit up, my curls sliding over the goose bumps on my shoulders. I try to watch him walk away but can no longer make out his outline amidst the gloom.

I could go back to my family. I could warm my skin by the hearth and wrap Jasper in a hug. Hear my father play his fiddle. I could find Draven and tell him that though his falcon died, I haven't. But doing all of this would mean admitting failure. Surrendering to starvation.

My heart is still beating fast so I make the best of it. Gathering up the hem of the dress, I dart into the forest. The animal in me screams not to turn my back on the candles of Morrot, but I ignore it and press through the shadows.

The dead and dying branches and shrubs of the woods are shredding the lace of my mother's dress. Something deep inside is tugging me forward and I know I am headed in the right direction. I continue at a jog and once or twice slip on ice, but pick myself up and keep going for what feels like miles.

To comfort myself as I plunge further into the woods, I remember how Scarlet used to come home from her lessons with the most wonderful tales. I would sit on the hearth with baby Jasper in my lap while she acted the stories out, her raven-dark hair flying behind her as she spun in mock battles and dances and tales of true love. In many of those times, we forgot about the darkness and felt only the light and warmth of home.

I stop running. If I turn my head from side to side, I can glimpse a dim glow through the ash and birch trees. By the time I reach the source of the light, I can't control my shivering. What I glimpse through the tree trunks makes me pause and hide myself. There before me is something I never expected. The light is not coming from a bonfire or even a cabin, but a two-storied mansion.

Its windows are all lit by candles and lamps, glowing warmly. I have never seen such a stately home. It is constructed of beams and planks, not logs. Despite the peeling paint, the front porch is so elegant with its buttresses and steepled roof that it takes a while before I realize I've been staring.

It is so out of place compared to the suffering of our village that it feels surreal, which is how I know it is his. I have to keep blinking as my eyes adjust to the light. Despite its cheerily lit windows, the house feels anything but happy. I can hear whispering from someone inside. The same voice I've heard before on the outskirts of the woods. Him.

I climb the stairs and open the door and the whispers stop as soon as I turn the knob. Whatever lies within knows I am here now.

Stepping inside, I close the door behind me and wait in the entryway as my skin thaws and my eyes adjust. It's not much warmer in the house, but at least the roof keeps out the moisture.

The interior is poorly lit. Placing all of the oil lamps and candles in the windows does little to illuminate the rooms I glimpse from where I stand. To my left is a parlor, to my right, a dining room and beyond that, what appears to be a kitchen. The darkness pooling in the middle of the rooms is eerie. I try to reason with myself that it's no different than the darkness outside, but I know that's a lie. This darkness is charged with threat.

"Hello?" I call.

My voice echoes throughout the rooms. Holding my breath, I listen but there isn't a single noise in response. But someone had to light the candles and lamps.

Like a child, I'm convinced the Bringer will pop out and frighten me. I let my irritation over the idea grow, coating my senses with armor.

"I know you're here," I say, quieter this time.

Then I hear it. A quiet scratching like a rodent or the rustle of fabric. Someone is moving away from me, hidden in the shadows. I grab the candle nearest me and thrust it forward. The sounds cease.

The first thing that I notice is a shape. Grotesque and distended by the flickering light, it is a hunched man on the stairway. Only it isn't his body on the stairs, I realize. It's his shadow, which means...

I spot him clinging to the wall. I hardly have time to register the red, gnarled flesh of his back when he scurries up the wall like a spider then leaps off of the banister, disappearing into the shadows above.

Gasping, I drop the candle, spilling hot wax on my thawing toes, making me shriek. Men don't move like that. This fiend defies gravity.

My heart is hammering so loudly that I can hear it in my ears like a drum again. I have to remind myself why I am here. I think of Jasper's smiling eyes. I think of the scent of my mother's skin. Father's hands. I think of Scarlet whispering to me that I knew what I had to do.

I listened to her, not because she could read and was smarter than me. But because when my sister told me she believed in me, it was after Elias had announced his plan for a sacrifice. When my sister was already dead.

Chapter Three

Biting my lip, I keep my eyes on the patch of wall where he disappeared as I bend down to retrieve the candle. The creature slipped into one of the rooms upstairs, and I'm not eager to follow. Now I know why I couldn't sense him at Sacrifice Rock. I can hear the spirits of the dead, but this creature isn't dead. In fact, I am now sure it once stalked Draven.

The few hunters who still venture out saw something shortly after the darkness stole our days completely. Draven was among them, and he described a man-like shape moving just beyond the light of their lanterns. The brief glimpse he'd had of the creature's flesh revealed skin gnarled and red, like tree bark. They were certain they had seen the Bringer. They tried to shoot him but he darted about with inhuman speed and escaped. Inhuman.

Just like whatever climbed up the wall. But someone in this house *is* dead. Otherwise I wouldn't have heard anything, and Scarlet wouldn't have said that I could help. She knew about my gift.

Whispers from the dead most often come just as we are about to sleep and are between dreaming and waking. The veil between our minds and spirits grows thin and we hear things that jolt us awake. Most don't remember what they heard, but as a Listener, I always remember. Even when I want to forget. And if I can hear a spirit, I can help it move on and find peace. I had thought the Bringer would be no different.

I'm alone in the entryway and the spilled wax has hardened on my slippers. The creature hasn't hurt me, though he has had plenty of occasions to, so I try to pretend he isn't hiding upstairs. Instead, I focus on the spirit in the house to find out what it wants. Its voice was the same as the one I've heard before in the woods, so I know it is linked to the shadows.

The chamberstick illuminates the room to my right as I shuffle towards it. The train of my dress is heavy with forest debris but I let it drag behind me, anchoring me to this world. The air is musty, rat and mice droppings are scattered on the floor, and the peeling wallpaper is speckled with mold. In the kitchen, I find a knife and suddenly feel less exposed.

A shriek sounds upstairs and the shock of the noise makes me stumble. It sounds like a man having his organs ripped out. My heart is hammering so much that my arms are shaking even as the scream fades. Then something shuffles before all is quiet again.

Is it the creature?

I take a moment to calm down before continuing.

Heading over to the foot of the staircase, I gather up my dress. Though my step is light, each stair still creaks with my footfalls. I find myself on a landing facing a hallway, my knife at the ready. Three doors line the wall with a fourth at the end of the hall. All are closed. The creature must be hiding behind one of them.

I hold still and listen for several moments. Though the house makes several quiet sounds as the wood settles, I don't hear any more moaning.

"Hello?" I whisper.

No one answers and I can't sense any sort of presence. The thought of the creature leaping out at me or shrieking, frightening me again, makes me bristle. As a Listener, I can't always control how I feel. Sometimes the dead ambush me with their emotions and it takes a lot of fighting to push them out. So if there's one thing I hate, it's when my own feelings run rampant.

Grabbing the knob on the first door, I yank it open and thrust my candle and knife inside. It's a room with a fireplace, a desk, a bookcase, and a bed. I linger in the doorway, sweeping every corner with my eyes, making sure the flickering light of the candle doesn't trick me into thinking I see something moving. Remembering how the creature had defied gravity, I check the ceiling and walls. Nothing's there but a water stained ceiling.

Stepping inside, I hold the light in the cavern of the fireplace and under the desk and bed, making sure he isn't hiding somewhere. He must be in another room, so I leave the door open and slip out. I scan the hallway and what I can see of the downstairs to make sure I am alone before I continue.

The second door is difficult to open, like it has been stuck for years. I briefly wonder if the creature has shoved something in front of it to keep me out. The idea of a beast being frightened of me almost makes me smile. The door suddenly gives and as I tumble within, something grabs my hair.

I panic and slash with the knife. A thin, sticky substance coats my hands and wrist. I realize that I have been trapped by spider webs, nothing more. I feel so stupid that I actually do smile now.

There's no need to step further into this room to know that it's empty. The floor is covered in rat droppings and abandoned nesting material from elsewhere in the house, but nothing anyone could hide behind or under. I check the ceiling again and take a moment to admire just how many spiders have made their home here. I've never seen such a billowing, dusty curtain above me.

Two doors left. I leave this one open and keep going. The third door is stuck, like the second, and that alone tells me that the creature isn't in here. I would've heard the racket these doors cause.

Leaving a trail of open rooms, I face the fourth and final door at the end of the hall. I slowly step towards it, readjusting my grip on the knife. Yet even in the shifting light of the candle, I can tell that it is not like the others. This door has something wrapped around the handle: chains.

The chains and key and even the doorknob are all so dusty that I know it hasn't been disturbed in ages. The creature couldn't have used it. So if he wasn't in any of the rooms upstairs and he wasn't downstairs, where was he?

I reach out to wipe at the dust to see how thick it is on the knob. I only have time to be surprised by the coldness of the metal. So cold that it's hot. Then the door starts rattling and banging.

Whatever is behind it is trying to get out. Suddenly I'm filled with anger that isn't mine. I yank my hand back and drop the knife. Sprinting, I race down the hallway. Each open door slams shut as I pass it. Painful, echoing claps. The chained door is still rattling as I reach the stairs.

My hand slips on the railing. I fall, bouncing down several steps until I manage to stop my descent with my right foot. My ankle erupts in fire and I know I've twisted it. The chamberstick has fallen to the bottom of the stairs and the candle is going out. My landing is hard and coughs the air from my lungs.

The flame is flickering and all of the lanterns and candles lining the windows are snuffing out. One by one. Closer and closer to me.

I try to yank myself onto my feet but keep getting caught in the hem of the long dress. I hear it tear, feel a draft up my thighs, and start moving. The house is now completely dark and the candle is flickering. I reach the door and grab the handle, twisting. Nothing happens. It's locked from the outside.

I am trapped. Then the candle dies.

My ankle is throbbing and my side is starting to hurt where I smacked my ribs on my fall. Leaning against the sticky wall for support, I straighten, taking weight off my ankle. I was foolish to have tried to run. Where did I think I'd go? The woods? Home?

"Stupid," I curse at myself. "Stupid, stupid, stupid..."

That's when I realize the foreign anger within me has left. It disappeared as I fell down the stairs. So whatever frustration I'm feeling now is mine.

The air around me starts to charge. I don't know if it's something only Listeners can sense, but I can feel it getting colder, too. So cold that the hair on my arms stands on end. I can detect something moving closer in the dark, something that I wouldn't be able to see even with the lights on. Because you can't see the dead. Sometimes people think they do, but it's only an image. Their mind making sense of a spirit's presence by painting a person.

And I feel whatever it is step right up to me. My chest gets tight and I can't breathe while it lingers in front of me. I've never had this strong of a reaction before. It moves past me, into the dining room. Once it is several feet away, I can breathe again.

Moistening my lips, I try to take a few steps towards it. My ankle throbs and I whimper. I wouldn't make it back home even if the door was unlocked. Quieting my mind, I listen for the presence in the other room. By stilling my own thoughts into the surface of a quiet pond, I invite the dead into my being. I am open, ready to listen, but the only emotion I can feel from the other room is a strange sort of indifference.

"I'm here to listen," I say quietly. "I'm not here to hurt you. I just want to help you."

All the lamps and candles in the house light so suddenly that I flinch. And it's not just the ones in the windows, it's sconces on the walls that I hadn't noticed before, with glass so coated in dust that they give off an eerie orange glow, as if the air is foggy. I only can barely wonder at the strength of this spirit before I hear shuffling in the other room. At first, I'm sure it's a rodent. But then it becomes clear that it's footsteps.

My back is against the wall and I'm balancing on one foot. I don't even have the candle to defend myself with. The floorboards creak as the thing comes closer and closer. The air around me is growing charged again, tugging at the tips of the hairs on my arms.

Don't be frightened, I chant over and over in my head. *Don't be frightened.*

A weight forms in my chest as the creaking footsteps draw nearer. Then they stop.

For the span of several heartbeats, there isn't a sound. Then I notice something on the ground out of the corner of my eye. It's dark and I can't make it out until I turn my head, and when I do, I have to bite my lip. It's a toenail. A ridged, yellowed, toenail attached to a browned foot, darkened by rotting.

Something leans around the entryway, peering at me. After the sight of the toe, I don't want to see the rest, but I force myself to look up. The first impression I have is of hair billowing underwater. Black funerary shrouds flutter in the air about a corpse.

It's a woman. Clumps of her hair are still sticking to her skull, dangling long past her waist. I wish the fabric was thicker, for through her veil I can glimpse dark eye sockets, a half-attached nose, and long teeth. They look large because there are no longer any lips to cover them. Jewelry adorns the woman's neck and one of her wrists, and her finery tells me she is the corpse of the spirit of the house.

Chapter Four

Rattling comes from within her chest as she shuffles to stand in front of me. Her rotting flesh should stink, but it doesn't. I remind myself that she can't smell because she can't really have a body. The dead can't reanimate their corpses. Or so I thought.

The heaviness grows in my chest as she leans forward. Her head tilts up and down, surveying me through eyes that melted long ago. How can she see me? How can she experience the world without her senses?

Don't be frightened, I chant again, even as the corpse lets out a wheeze in front of me. *She's only an apparition. She can't hurt me. She can't –*

Her hand reaches into the folds of her shrouds and pulls out a thin strand of pearls. They're ivory and elegant as they slither through her rotting fingers. I realize those pearls might have something to do with what's troubling her. I force steadiness into my voice.

"They're beautiful," I whisper.

A bony hand darts forward and clamps on both of my wrists like a shackle. I cry out in surprise at her strength and can't breathe at all as she leans her skull in to mine. A rattling exhalation blows the hair off my face as she slides the pearls around my wrists, like a snake. They're smooth, almost like liquid, and their sensation is so pleasant and her eyeless sockets are so near that it takes me too long to realize that she's binding my hands together. I try to move my arms to get away but the heaviness in me is so strong that I can't budge.

Her funerary shrouds brush against my mother's wedding dress. Wheezing comes out from behind her teeth, accompanied with squeaking, and I realize she's trying to speak.

"Special?" She hisses as the pearls get tighter. "You think you're special?'

I part my lips but I can't respond. It's like my lungs are locked in ice.

The pearls clutched in one hand, she traces my jaw with the forefinger of the other. Her skull tilts to the side as a wheeze-like a growl rumbles in her chest.

"Not so special anymore."

She lets go and though she isn't touching me, my wrists are yanked above my head. I scream out the last of my air as my elbows are nearly wrenched out of socket. Only the tips of my toes can touch the ground. The lights begin to snuff out and the corpse disappears, dissolving into the darkness until she is one with the shadows. The weight in my chest fades and I take several strangled breaths.

I am in total darkness once again.

My ankle is pulsing furiously now but I put weight on it anyway. I try to balance as I yank at my bonds but they are held fast to something above me that I can't even see. Grunting as I try to free myself, I only wind up swaying from side to side, so I hold still and dangle like an animal in a snare.

"Let me go," I scream so loud that it vibrates in the back of my throat. My demand echoes through the house. There is no response. That's when I notice the cold again. I can't even hug myself for warmth.

When minutes slip past and there is no sign of stirring within the house, my pulse slows. Maybe the spirit wanted me here so that I could die. Starvation while my limbs feel like they are slowly tearing at the joints. The cold is numbing me now, slipping up the tear in my dress so that I have no warmth.

Tears escape as I think of Jasper. I try to remember his smiling eyes, but every time I start to see them, they fade. I worry I'll never be able to remember them. Instead, I can see Draven's eyes perfectly. They're so clear that I allow myself to slip inside of them, into memory of a time with the sun.

Draven and I were ten. We lay side by side on our stomachs, the hay beneath us prickling our skin through our clothes. In front of us, nestled in otter fur, was a small egg. Though the chick inside had been pipping for some time, the egg had yet to open more than a short crack on the side.

"Tell me the story of how you got it again," I murmured, my chin resting on my folded arms.

Draven shifted to sit up and began tearing at a piece of straw. His blonde curls were streaked with brown and matted together behind his head, like they always were back then. He was afraid of brushes.

"I snuck out a few weeks ago with my bow and quiver," he said.

The sunlight was pouring into the window of his barn, filling the air with the scent of warm hay. The chickens lived inside during the winter snow, but since it was summer, they were out scratching under bushes elsewhere, leaving us in peace. The light haloed Draven's messy hair, so golden against the sunkissed tan of his skin.

"Did your mother know you were gone?" I asked, rolling onto my side. The egg wasn't showing more signs of progress. Draven was more interesting.

"No, I left before she was awake. I walked for hours. So long that my boots were rubbing my feet raw in places."

"Then what happened?" I asked. Draven was quiet by nature and had a habit of drifting off into thought if I didn't prompt him. My mother said he was a little daft. Megan liked to tease him, calling him mute. He was neither of those things. He just didn't waste breath.

"I came to the base of a cliff," he continued, knotting his piece of hay. "It was taller than the tallest trees. But that's where the nest was. So I took off my gear and boots and started to climb."

"Did you fall?"

He shook his head. "I slipped. And cut myself open a bunch. And I couldn't look down. About halfway up, I reached this sort of grassy place that was flat so I climbed onto it. From there I could hike the rest of the way up to the top."

"And that's when you realized the nest was below you?" I asked. I'd heard this story several times before, but I loved listening to stories back then. I still do, when they're not whispered by strangers, that is.

Draven nodded and looked at me, casting aside his piece of straw. His angel bow lips smiled. "About five lengths down."

"Lengths of your body, you mean."

He nodded. "I lay on my belly and looked over the edge and could see four brown eggs in the nest. The parents probably couldn't raise all those chicks anyway."

I smiled. This part was my favorite. When Draven would look at me as he told it, I would feel this tingly warmth on the back of my neck, like the sunlight. Because all of the color in his eyes was focused on me. Just me. And I had time to try to hunt out his pupils amidst all that dark brown.

"So then I was able to use this rope that I'd brought. I tied it to the trunk of a tree at the top—"

"A stump," I corrected.

"Yeah, a stump, because it was closest to the edge. Then I tied the other end around my waist and started to lower myself down. Then the rope started feeling floppy and all the sudden I slipped. I grabbed onto a tree root," he mimicked grabbing something in the air before him, "and could hear all these rocks falling. I was able to climb back up the root and saw that the rope had slid off the stupid stump. It had crumbled in from termites and stuff."

"You would've died."

Draven nodded. "So this time, I was more careful. I tied the rope to a tree trunk, even if it was farther away. I didn't have enough rope left to tie it around my waist and still reach the nest, so instead I just wrapped it around my wrists and slid."

I eyed the scarring marks on his knuckles and palms. He hadn't been able to use his crossbow for over a week.

"The rope burned really bad, but I slid until my feet touched the ledge the nest was on. I picked the biggest egg and tucked it into my shirt, like this."

He slipped his hand under his sleeveless tunic and rested it against the left side of his chest. As if in response, the egg started pipping again.

"Then I had to climb back up. That was the hardest part because my hands hurt so bad and were bleeding. It took a long time but I made it to the top. I just walked all the way down the other side of the cliff – the part that was a slope on the other side of the mountain. It took me until nighttime to reach my gear again but it was better than trying to climb down the face."

"And safer." I started to braid three pieces of straw together.

"Yeah. The egg was still warm against my skin so I hurried home. The moon was bright so I didn't get lost. I got in a lot of trouble when I got home until I showed my parents the egg."

"Then what did they do?" I handed the braided straw to Draven, who wound it around his wrist.

"My father wrapped it in his otter pelt since it's the warmest." He tried to tie another piece of straw around the braid to secure it, but it was hard with one scabbed hand. "Then my mother slipped it all under a broody hen. She pecked her lots but warmed the egg like it was hers."

He was still struggling with fastening his bracelet so I sat up and tied it for him. That was when I saw the egg move out of the corner of my eye. "Draven, look."

We fell onto our bellies and nearly held our breath as we watched the brown speckled egg. After several moments, it moved again and the crack on the side widened. Draven giggled. "I knew it. Today's the day!"

"Shh," I hushed. "Don't scare the baby."

We watched as quietly as we could as the egg slowly hatched. The crack grew bigger and bigger and once the shell started to separate, we could glimpse the pink body of the chick. Draven only left once to get his father, Lucian. When the beak was peeking out and the chick was almost free, Lucian slapped Draven on the back. "Pick it up, boy!"

Draven's eyes grew. "Me?'

Lucian grabbed the bundle and shoved it into his son's hands. "She's yours."

I laughed then because Draven was smiling so much, and his smile was the biggest I'd ever seen. So big that his eyes narrowed and deep lines curved at the sides of his mouth. It always made me smile back. He cradled the bundle in his arms as the little bird fought its way out. It was wet and weak, covered with white feathers that looked like clumps of thin fur. Its eyes were still closed, but I knew that once it could glimpse the outside world, Draven's smile would be the first thing it would see. From that point onwards, he and the falcon were inseparable.

He named her Lady.

A light appears at the top of the stairs and I am yanked back into the present. I spent so long in my imagination that I wonder if I was sleeping. The only sensation left in my arms is a cold, aching pain. The light at the top of the stairs is a candle's flame, and it flickers as it slowly moves downwards.

It's either floating or held by someone but I am too tired to be afraid. Still, I brace myself for the ugly sight of the woman's corpse again. But as the candle nears, casting flickering light, I glimpse a vest and trousers. The candle is held by a man.

Not just any man, I realize as he nears and I can make out the features of his face. He is the most handsome man I have ever seen.

Chapter Five

His skin is smooth and olive, and even in the flickering light I can tell that it is nearly without flaw. He is young, maybe only a few years older than me. His hair and eyes are dark, his lips slightly downturned at the corners though his expression is relaxed. Pleasant. He is of slight build, as if he has never had to toil in much physical labor, and combined with the air of effortless nobility that clings to him, I know he is the true owner of this house.

I don't know where he has been all this time. I don't know why he has come to me now. Those questions are suddenly unimportant. He pauses before me, the candlelight reflecting in his almond-shaped eyes.

"Hello," he says softly with a shy smile, making the flame jitter.

Setting the sconce on the floor a ways away, he reaches up to my bound wrists. I lick my lips to tell him that it's no use and that they're rock solid, but before I can, he has freed me.

My weight is suddenly returned to my feet and my bad ankle. My arms are like lead and useless and my heart skips a beat as I fall. But he catches me, his arms cradling my back. Blood rushes into my limbs, and it is warm and awful. The candlelight illuminates the side of his face. Such dark eyes set into elegant, broad cheekbones. He holds me, nearly lateral for several seconds before picking me up.

Leaving the chamberstick behind, he slowly climbs the stairs. My limbs are so numb that I can hardly feel the heat from his body, but his heart beats slow and steady against my side. We reach the first door in the hall upstairs and he shoulders it open before entering. I can't see anything in the dark but he lowers me onto what feels like the bed. Lying still, I let the blood rush about my aching bones. I tentatively lift my right arm as I hear him cross the room. It hurts but I can command it once again. I try my left and start bending my knees while I hear him scraping around. After a minute or two, he lights a fire.

The flames cast bright light around the small room and I have to blink until my eyes adjust. This is the room with the desk and the books. Half of his body is silhouette, as if painted by shadows, but they aren't frightening. They highlight his curves and angles and I find myself staring because he is pleasant to look at. After a while I realize he is likewise staring at me. A light flush stirs inside.

"You are warm," he says. His voice is husky and tinted with a whisper, like it fades around the edges of his words.

"I am cold," I answer, my voice squeaking a little. My throat is dry and my lips are cracking. It has been a long time since I last ate or drank.

His placid expression doesn't change as he continues to study me. Then, as if rousing himself from his thoughts, he gestures to the fire. "This will warm you." He strides towards the door. "I will return. Do not leave this room."

I nod. I am captivated by his voice. It is both deep and shallow, lyrical and flat. I wonder if it is actually quite normal and if I am losing my grip on reality. I need to eat and sleep. This should feel strange to me, but it doesn't. It feels welcome.

He has closed the door behind him and I let the warmth from the fire thaw me before I try out my legs. After sliding to the edge of the bed, I press my slipper toes against the floor. Holding onto one of the bedposts, I balance on my good leg for a moment then hobble over to the fire. The snap and hiss of the heat digging into pine makes me smile. Fire is warm and welcoming. Fire is hearth and home.

The man returns with a jug and a goblet that's still damp, as if he has just washed it. He pours me some water and it's cool and sweet. The moment it hits my tongue, I realize how parched I am. I drink glass after glass and the jug is nearly empty before I am satiated.

"Who are you?" I ask, my voice steady now.

"Who are you?" He sets the pitcher and cup on the desk.

"Willow. From the village of Morrot. My father is a merchant. Or... he was."

He is lingering by the desk, in the shadows. The contrast of his clean, white collared shirt beneath his black vest makes me wonder what I must look like. My mother's wedding dress is tattered and torn and a slit now stretches up to my hip at the side. I close the top of the gap with my hand. For a moment, I feel shame, but when I look back at him his expression is still placid, as if he hasn't noticed. "Do you live here?"

He cocks his head slightly. "Do you?"

"No."

"But you're here now."

His questioning is so simple that I wonder if he really understands me. Maybe I'm not speaking his first language. "Only for a little while," I say back.

A corner of his mouth lifts in a faint smirk. The first true emotion he has shown. "How long is a little while?"

I sigh and rub my face with my hands. In the firelight, I am surprised to find that they're grimy. The house has dirtied me. "I don't know. However long it takes, I suppose."

"However long what takes?"

"Helping the dead in this house."

His amusement fades.

"The woman who hanged me... the... corpse. I came here to help her."

Sorrow flashes in his eyes, making him look so horribly vulnerable that my breath hitches in my lungs. He shakes off his stillness and crosses over to me. Kneeling by the fire, he studies it before looking me in the eye. "Don't hunt for her."

"Why?"

He rests his cool hand on mine, his gaze earnest. "Promise me you won't."

"All right. I won't."

The smile is back and he looks at our hands. "You're warmer."

"Thank you for the fire."

He squeezes my hand then rises. "Rest here. I'll bring you something to eat."

I nod as he heads for the door. "Thank you."

He pauses with his back to me then looks over his shoulder with a whimsical expression. "I feel it but I don't recall the word."

"Thank you?" I ask.

"No…" Then he grins with realization. "Welcome." He looks me in the eye. "You're welcome."

I smile. He slips back out and now I am sure that he hasn't spoken my language in a long time. His mind is so rusty that I wonder if he has spent years in isolation with only a dead woman for company. And a creature.

Where has the creature been hiding all this time? It seemed skittish. Maybe it's back out in the woods. The Bringer would wander the woods. But what did he have to do with the corpse?

Her aggression is as unusual as her still having a body. Dead strangers often tell me their secrets then barrage me with anger. Unlike the corpse, it isn't anger directed at me. It is anger over what they did or didn't do in life.

Grandma Abella was a Listener, as well. She must have been more sensitive than I am. The only way the dead can speak to us is by whispering and making us experience what they feel. Bearing all that remorse inside is not natural. That's why she jumped off a cliff.

I wait for the man by the fire, but when he doesn't return soon and my ankle keeps throbbing, I get up and hobble to the bed. The covers haven't been washed in a while but they are warm. I slip underneath and wish I had something more comfortable to wear. I try to stay awake to wait for him, but I am sleepy. I imagine that the warmth I feel is from the sun, like it was the day everything changed.

It was late summer. Scarlet and I were picking blackberries by the river. Our mother used the juice to dye the fabrics my father sold, but she always left enough for us to eat until we were sick. I was fourteen and though my sister was only three years older than me, she looked like a lady. She had our mother's cheekbones and father's black hair. In the sunlight, her eyes glimmered like blue jewels. Her body was lithe and tall, unlike mine, and I wished I looked more like her. Sometimes I wished I was her.

"The woman turned into a horse," she said finishing recounting a tale she'd recently read as she plopped a handful of berries into the basket. The bottom was permanently stained purple from years of summers. The air was fresh with the scent of water, river mud and berries. A bird chattered loudly overhead. The earth offered such simple joys back then. "And was never seen again."

"Just wait until I can share my own stories," I said with a grin. I'd been holding this news inside the whole length of her recounting.

"What do you mean?" She stained her temple with berry juice as she brushed back a curl, turning to look at me.

I picked a thorn out of my thumb with my teeth while raising my brows. "Elias asked me to come learn. He wants to teach me to read, as well!"

Scarlet didn't even smile as she gently lifted a clump of leaves to reveal a clutch of ripe berries underneath where the birds hadn't yet spotted them.

I swallowed and watched her profile. "Scarlet?"

"You already *have* your own stories," she said in a rush, facing me. "Like the one where you tried to throw that rock in the well when you were six and you were filled with the thoughts of the boy who'd drowned doing the same thing."

Scarlet had let the basket slide from the crook of her arm to her purple hand. Neither of us was picking berries anymore.

"That's not the same," I complained.

"It's far better. What about when I was asleep and Grandma was talking to you after she died and you said she kept getting her words mixed up, like she couldn't focus for long. Then you realized she was saying 'You are me.' That's better than anything I've ever read."

The bird overhead was still chattering loudly and for a moment, it was the only sound.

"I see," I whispered. "You don't want me to be as smart as you."

The berry she was picking burst in her fingers, staining them anew. "Of course not. Lil, you have a wonderful gift. Who needs to read when you can hear the spirits of the Netherworld?"

She linked her glistening red fingers with my purple ones and smiled, as if she was worried about something.

"Promise me you'll tell him no?"

Something was tugging on me deep behind her eyes, so I nodded. The bird chattering overhead took off. Once in the air, it screeched several times. A screech I knew well. It was Lady. And where Lady was, her master was never far behind.

"Draven!" I hissed.

Scarlet squawked as he popped up from behind the berry bushes several yards downstream. His lips were stained purple and his expression was contrite, a half-finished necklace in his hands.

"What're you doing here?" I demanded.

He didn't have time to answer before Scarlet started pelting him with berries. He held up his arms to block them as he made his way over. "You snitch!" she hissed. "You sneaky little stalker!"

"Hey," he shouted, but Scarlet didn't let up her assault and by the time Draven reached us, he looked like he was bleeding from multiple arrow wounds.

I glared at him and he shifted his weight uncomfortably. "Is it true?"

Scarlet was about to hurl an entire handful of berries at him but subdued herself at his question. I nodded my head at her, approving of the cease-fire. I looked back to Draven.

His eyes are dark like soil, yet always hold a warm, hearth-like ember.

I tensed as his gaze stripped away my body, worrying that he would be frightened, but instead, the ember glowed all the brighter. "How beautiful," he whispered, so softly that we could hardly hear him.

"What is that, anyway?" I snapped, peering at the necklace in his hands as the glow in his eyes made my chest heat up in response.

"It's for my father," he said, holding up the string of beads and molted falcon feathers from Lady. "To protect him against the shadow when he goes into the woods."

Scarlet and I exchanged a tight look, for the darkness in the forest was something we liked to pretend wasn't real.

"I best be off then," Draven said with a small smile before imitating a falcon's cry and holding out his arm. Lady swooped through the meadow then landed on the leather that was always wrapped around his wrist to protect his skin from her hunter's talons.

He inclined his head at both of us then jogged back towards the village. In the distance, I could see Lucian outside his house, lacing up his boots as he prepared to leave.

I never had to ask Draven to keep my secret, just as I didn't have to ask what had happened when I awoke to him wailing a few days later. The necklace hadn't worked. Lucian's body was found at the base of a hill after he lost his footing high above. Draven made himself scarcer than ever after that, until the harvest festival.

His mother muttered to mine that he hadn't spoken in weeks. Across the field of bonfires and dancing families and couples, we gazed at each other. The drums pulsed. He crossed over to me, holding an orange and yellow leaf by the stem. I opened my mouth to say something but he tucked the leaf in my hair, adding it to my autumn crown. He didn't need to speak. I could tell what he was thinking by looking into his eyes.

I led Draven over to a corner where there was just enough firelight to see each other's faces. We sat down and I held his hand in both of mine, resting in my lap. I waited for him to ask if I'd ever heard his father, or if I knew where he was, but he didn't say anything.

After some time, his shoulders started to shake and he sobbed. I didn't try to hug him as he cried. He had his pride and that would only push him away, so I held his calloused hand, his knuckles white. I sat with him until he was finished.

Then he squeezed my fingers and muttered something about checking on Lady. I waited until I couldn't see him anymore then headed back to the field. Scarlet was waiting for me, sitting on a bale of hay on the rim of firelight. She watched me intently as I sat down beside her.

"What?" I asked.

"I don't think spirits have to be dead for you to hear them," she whispered.

I blushed and smiled at the same time. Scarlet hugged me and kissed the top of my head. She smelled like apples.

I wake up from my own drool staining the pillow and coating my cheek. The fire has died down to ash and its dim embers are the only light in the room.

Hobbling over to the window, I peer outside. I can't tell if I'm looking at sky or trees which either means it's day or cloudy night. What I miss the most about mornings are the birds. I loved to lie in bed, toasty beside Scarlet, and listen to their songs. Are there any birds left? Certainly not here. Draven snuck portions of his meat to Lady whenever he could, yet even so, she died.

Limping over to the fireplace, I find some small branches on the hearth. After prodding the embers, the fire comes to life and I sit beside it, using the light to examine my ankle. It's swollen and purpling but I've seen worse. I just wish it would heal faster.

The house creaks and at first I think it's the man returning, but it's just the wood settling. Here on the hearth, it's hard to imagine that this is the same house that tormented me yesterday. Or at least, what feels like yesterday. For all I know, it was two or three days ago.

The hours slip past and I grow restless. I keep my ankle elevated and the fire burning, but I am hungry and bored. The bookcase beside the desk is full of books, and if I could read, I could entertain myself for days and days in here. Part of me wants to get this over with and leave the room. Look for the dead woman and help her leave this place to see if she takes the Bringer with her. But the young man told me not to leave the room, so I stay.

I feel like it has been a full day by the time I hear any movement in the house. The stairs begin to creak with footsteps. One after another. My pulse picks up, making my ankle throb as I worry it's her. Then the doorknob turns and I see a white shoulder entering. I actually smile in relief. He has come back, and with him are two dead, skinned rats.

"I'm so hungry," I say.

He skewers a rat and begins roasting it in the flames. "They're both for you."

I'm once again struck by how much I enjoy looking at his face. He is concentrating on cooking so I feel free to stare for several moments. The hollow of his cheeks suck in a little, as if he has lost any trace of baby fat. That's not surprising. With the hunger in our woods, all of us have. "What's your name?"

He blinks as he looks to me, his lips parted in surprise. "I… I don't know." His voice is soft but firmer than before.

"What do you mean you don't know?"

"I've been here so long that I've forgotten."

"So you do live here?"

He nods. His dark hair is straight, for the most part. A few strands have fallen into his face. I'm tempted to brush them away to better see his eyes but keep my hands to myself.

"Why didn't I see you earlier?" I ask.

"Earlier?"

"I explored the whole house when I got here."

"Not the whole house."

Fair enough. In the darkness I could have missed a cubby or a servant's entrance. "You must be very lonely here all by yourself."

He stops rotating the rat. I've never seen a grown man look so much like a wounded little boy. "I am so lonesome."

I rest my hand on his shoulder and squeeze. He is cool. He must've been waiting a long time in the cold to trap the rats. "Why are you sad?"

"You will leave," he whispers.

I catch myself watching the reflection of the fire in his eyes for far too long. I will leave. Yes, I will. And go back home. To my family. How could I have forgotten that? "You live with the dead woman?"

He nods.

"And the creature? That walks on walls?"

He nods again, a thin line forming between his brows.

"My friend Megan used to wake up to weeping when no one was there, so I spent the night. The spirit of her grandmother was trapped in her sorrow. She thought her daughter was ill. So I welcomed her into me and showed her that her daughter was well. There hasn't been any weeping since. I could do the same with –"

"It's too dangerous."

I don't have it in me to argue at the moment. "Why don't you leave?"

He sighs and pulls the first rat out, inspecting it. The scent of the warm flesh and sizzling grease make my stomach contract. I'd put the whole thing in my mouth if I could. But it isn't done enough so he sticks it back in.

"How can I go anywhere," he says softly. "When I don't even have a name?"

"Then I'll give you one," I say, squeezing his shoulder. A name is so quickly on my tongue that I wonder if I've been waiting to say it all along. "Tristan. I will call you Tristan."

He slowly smiles. "Tristan," he says, trying it out. "It suits me. You're welcome, Willow."

"No," I say with a smile. "It's thank you."

He chuckles. "Yes, thank you, Willow."

His charm is so childlike that I find myself forgetting the darkness when he is beside me like he is now.

Just then, there is a bang down the hall as the chained door starts rattling.

Chapter Six

Tristan leaps to his feet, his shoulders stiff as he stares at our door.

My palms are pressed against the hearth, ready to move if I have to. "What is she?"

"Angry."

The chained door stops banging and I smell something burning and hastily grab the cooked rat out of the fire. "I don't understand," I say. "Anything. This house. Her. You."

He looks at me over his shoulder. "I must go."

I yank myself up onto my good foot. "No, you mustn't. Not till I have some answers."

He shakes his head, his eyes helpless. "I cannot linger. I've tarried too long already. She is coming."

I'm suddenly not hungry anymore. The hair on the back of my neck and arms stands on end. "Why?"

He blinks several times, studying the floorboards, as if listening to something distant. "I think she means to kill you."

"What?" I snap.

"You upset her."

"But she was whispering. When I first got here, I heard her. The only spirits who whisper are the ones that want help. That want to let go."

He shakes his head. "She doesn't want to let go of anything, that's the problem." He gasps and grabs at the left side of his chest, as if he's been hurt.

I take a wobbly step forward, holding onto the mantle for support. "Tristan?"

"I have to go," he chokes out. I can't tell if he's trying not to cry or if he's having trouble breathing. He grabs something from his breast pocket and presses it into my palm. It's icy cold. "You should be safe here. I have claimed this space. She cannot form inside. Don't let her in."

"What's happening?" I shout.

He pivots to face me, his hand still over his heart. For the first time, his eyes glimmer with something dark. "She's hurting me."

I can sense that she is still in the room at the end of the hall, behind the chained door. She's gaining strength but can't yet affect me. So why can she affect Tristan?

"How?" I ask, then shake my head. "Get away from her. Out of the house. Far away."

Tristan gasps again and his knees nearly buckle. I reach out to steady him but he shoves my hands away. "I can't," he chokes out.

"You can!"

"I'm her prisoner," he shouts. "She has attached herself to me. She..." The most horrible choking sound comes out of his throat instead of words.

Tristan fumbles with the knob and I am so unsettled by the noises he's making that I don't try to stop him. He slams the door shut behind him and I hobble over and listen. I look at my palm. He gave me a skeleton key. His footsteps echo as he runs, heading for the stairs. He makes it halfway down then stops. Why did he stop?

The tightness in my chest returns and I know she is back.

Thump.

Footfalls echo in the hall outside my door as she walks down it, heading for the stairs.

Thump.

Heading for Tristan.

I want to scream at her to leave him alone. I want to shout at him to run. But I don't understand what's going on and he does. Anything I do might make it worse for him. So instead, I lock my door with the key.

Thump.

The heaviness gets worse as the corpse passes my door. Her footsteps are on the stair, slowly descending.

Thump.

They pause where Tristan stopped.

For several moments, all I can hear is my own breathing.

Then he screams and it's so tortured that I shriek in response. Clamping a hand over my mouth, I lose my balance and fall. His scream morphs into a dying moan, like he has no air left. Then it suddenly cuts off.

I lie on the floor, a cold sweat on the back of my neck and chest. Over my rapid breaths, I can't hear anything.

Then they're back. The horrible footsteps.

Thump. Thump.

At first I think they're continuing down the stairs, and then I realize with a jolt that they're coming back up. They're moving faster now, too. They're already in the hall.

I scoot backwards, towards the fireplace. The thumping stops outside my door. I don't dare blink in the silence that follows. The fire hisses and snaps. It squeaks.

No, it's not the fire squeaking. It's the doorknob.

The brass fixture is slowly turning. My eyes dart to the burnt rat. Yanking it off the skewer, I hold the thin spear in front of me. The doorknob continues to turn. I scramble to my feet, my ankle burning. There's a click and I'm worried the latch has been released. The doorknob stills. Relief floods me. She has hit the lock. Tristan was right. She can't get in.

I lower the spear, but just then, the door bangs so loud that I scream again. It keeps on banging, rattling so hard in its frame that dust falls from the ceiling. I drop my weapon and cover my ears, falling to my knees, as if that would protect me.

The banging ceases and as I pull my hands away from my ears, I hear the rustle of fabric, then the thump of her footsteps as she heads back towards the stairs.

Red light comes through the thin crack at the bottom of the door. She must've lit the lamps and candles again. Why would she even care if they glowed? She can't see, anyway. At least, she has no eyes. Maybe she uses the lights as bait to lure prey like me into the house.

Climbing back to my feet, I sit on the hearth once more. I add more wood to the fire, even though it doesn't need it. I need it.

What did she do to Tristan? The memory of his screaming makes me feel sick to my stomach. What if she killed him?

It is some time before I have the nerves to do much of anything, but I force myself to eat the burnt rat. Skewering the other, I cook it for later. I should take it and run. Get as far away from this place as possible. The front door may be locked but I could break a window. And then there's wherever Tristan hides. Maybe there's an exit there.

Tristan. I can't leave without him. I'll have to convince him to run away with me, if he's even still alive.

I've never heard of a spirit having the strength to imprison someone before. Then again, I've never heard of a spirit inhabiting its corpse, either. What's she feeding off of to get the strength to slam doors and light candles? To bind me with iron force?

Then it hits me. It's Tristan. I don't know how or why but she must be siphoning off his life, like a leech. She keeps him prisoner so that she can continue to stalk about as a carcass in a gross mockery of life. Many are afraid of death, but to be satisfied with living as a corpse, torturing someone for energy, is beyond my comprehension.

As is how a dead woman could possibly suck energy out of a living man. To make a connection like that she would have to be able to enter his spirit. And as far as I know, the only way she could do that is if he's a Listener.

Maybe that's what she's been doing to me, too. Why I feel like I can't breathe while she's near. Maybe that's why she wants me. She'll suck all of the life out of me for herself then let me rot. I grab the skewer again. I'm not a sacrifice anymore.

I wait for hours, but I am not bored, I am on edge. Every once in a while there's a noise downstairs. The clatter of a pot. A thud. Sounds that could be caused by rats but could just as well be the corpse. Sounds that remind me that I am safe up here, and I don't want to leave the room anymore.

When there are footsteps on the stairs, I tense. I wait for the heavy feeling in my chest but it doesn't come. The steps are lighter, anyway, and relief calms me as I recognize them as Tristan's. He stops outside the door.

"Willow?"

I hobble over and unlock it, letting him in. He takes two steps then sags, collapsing in front of the fire. I fumble with the key, locking the door again as I look at him. The side of his face is slick with blood. Hurrying over to Tristan, I kneel at his side. "What happened?"

Gently brushing away his now unruly hair, I peer at his wound. The blood is coming from gouge marks in the side of his face. Tearing off a tattered piece of my dress, I press it against his temple. He winces at the touch. "I need the fire," he whispers. "I'm so cold."

I grab his hand. He isn't cold. He's freezing. I begin rubbing his back to help him warm up. My fingers slide over bumps that feel like his spine until I notice they're too far to the side. Rubbing my hand in a slow circle, I realize his back is covered in the lumps.

Something sour tugs at the bottom of my stomach as I realize what I'm feeling. Tristan's breathing hitches in his throat when my hand stops and he gazes at me. His eyes are asking me not to, but I un-tuck his shirt and loosen his vest so that I can see his back.

I close my eyes. It is the corded, red skin of the creature I glimpsed scurrying up the wall. Grabbing his wrist, I yank up his sleeve. Though his hands are untouched, his arms are the same. My eyes lock onto his. He is the Bringer.

Chapter Seven

Tristan's eyes are apprehensive. He holds the fabric against his cheek as I scoot away and study him long enough for the bleeding to stop. Clenching my teeth, I don't know if I'm angrier at him for being the cause of all our distress or at myself for having been foolish enough to have been wooed by a pretty face. To have trusted him.

"You're a monster," I whisper.

He can't hold my gaze anymore and looks away.

"Why?"

He shakes his head, his bangs curtaining his eyes.

"My people are starving. My family is going to die."

"We all die," he says softly, and I find nothing pleasant in his peculiar voice now.

"But you're not even giving us a chance."

Tristan looks at me, his dark eyes confused. "Me?"

"You're the Bringer of Darkness."

"No..."

"We've seen you in the woods. And that was you who touched me at Sacrifice Rock, wasn't it?"

He gingerly peels the fabric off of his wound. "Did they expect me to eat you?"

I narrow my eyes. "I was the sacrifice."

"Like the pig and cow?"

I nod.

He sneers. "Who would send their own daughter to die?"

I lick my lips. "No one sent me. I volunteered."

"Why?"

"I'm a Listener. I thought I could help you. Reason with you. Do something to get you to bring the light back. But that was before I knew you were also a Listener."

"Willow," he says thoughtfully, carefully setting the cloth on the hearth. "I may be beyond help, but I am not this Bringer of Darkness you speak of."

I lean my back against the foot of the bed. I feel like I don't speak anyone's language anymore for how little I understand. "Then who are you?"

A corner of his lips lifts in a smile. "I am Tristan."

I try not to let the simplicity of his charm infiltrate my logic again. "Who are you really?"

"I told you, I can't remember."

"How long have you been here?"

"Too long."

"Since you were a child?"

He shakes his head.

"Since before the darkness began?"

"Certainly."

I sigh. Getting answers out of him, in fact, even getting him to think is like trying to grab a slippery trout in a stream. I can't make sense of the creature climbing up the wall and the handsome young man before me. "Did you live here alone?"

"No. I was with my family."

"What happened to them?"

His eyes darken. "Death."

I furrow my brow. "Then... is the spirit in this house... is the corpse woman someone you knew?"

He nods, closing his eyes for a moment, as if he's exhausted, and I'm reminded that he is injured. That the corpse did something to him to make him scream so horribly earlier. And here I am, not giving him a moment's peace.

"I can't escape her," he says so quietly that his voice cracks. "I've tried."

When he opens his eyes, they're shimmering in the firelight and I realize he's holding back tears.

"I've tried so hard. But her grip upon me is as iron. We were once bonded by such affection but now..." Tristan shakes his head. "Now we are like a cat and mouse."

"What does she do to you?" I ask, even though I'm not sure I want to hear the answer.

He closes his eyes again and takes a deep breath. "She... feeds off of me. I used to not notice. It used to be gentle. But that was when her body was sound. Once decay set in... she fought against it as hard as she could. She should be bones. Now it hurts because she is doing something so unnatural. So grotesque. She needs more and more from me. And she often takes it in anger so that it hurts me more."

Tristan looks so broken, sitting slumped by the fire, blood staining his cheek, that I scoot over and hug him. He is still cool but not half as much as before. He doesn't move for several moments then slowly wraps his arms around me. When he leans in, his chest gently presses against mine and I feel him tremble.

"What is this?" he whispers.

"A hug."

"A hug... I remember hugs now."

He relaxes and I close my eyes. For several long moments, I listen to the fire and feel the tickling brush of his hair against my ear. He smells like autumn leaves and rain. Like the forest. My hand is resting on the lumps beneath his clothing and I remind myself that I saw him crawl on a wall once. Pulling away, I tilt my head to look him in the eye but am distracted when I notice that his wound is gone, leaving only dried blood on his cheek.

I shake my head. "What are you?"

He looks confused so I slide his sleeve back, revealing the red, gnarled skin there. He follows my gaze and sighs. "Burns."

"Did she do this to you?"

He nods, his hair falling into his face again.

"I know that as a Listener it's hard to block them out sometimes. But you need to try. Otherwise you'll never escape her."

"Oh, Willow," he says, pulling his arm out of my touch. "It's not like that. You see..."

He folds his sleeve all the way back to reveal the full extent of his scarring. I've never seen burns like this before. These look like there's no skin left. Only scars on muscle.

"I am not a Listener." Tristan rises and the fire suddenly snuffs down to embers. At the same moment, his scars fade away to smooth skin like his hands, rippled by a hidden vein.

I don't move. I have seen more in this house that would make me question my sanity than most people see in a lifetime. "Then what are you?"

His eyes take on that horrible sadness again. A sadness that is so vulnerable and pure and one-dimensional that I realize I already know what he is about to say.

"Not what. Why."

The coolness of his skin. The strength of his emotions. His attachment to the corpse. His simplicity. "You're dead," I whisper.

"No... but I am also not living. I am trapped in-between."

Chapter Eight

I am only just starting to understand the true nature of Tristan's imprisonment. It takes a while for what he has told me to sink in. In fact, I have to rework most of what I thought was true. I feel lost in my own mind. Like all of the walls of the world just started floating around and now I have to stick them back down in a new shape. A new shape that defies gravity. Like Tristan.

"Why?" I manage to whisper back, repeating him.

"Yes, why am I?" he asks, crouching a few feet before me. "Because there is no answer to what or how."

My head is empty except for a sort of wind that is fluttering about leaves that used to be thoughts. I notice how young and alive he looks, gazing at me. How much I want to touch his skin. Then I remind myself not to use him as an anchor. He isn't an anchor. He's an abomination.

Think of Jasper, I tell myself. And then I am filled with the memory of the scent of his head. Cradlecap and blankets. How little his hands and body are. How I am secretly happy that he is small because it means I can hold him all the longer. Hold him. I would hold him as I slept. Then I see Draven's face, gaunt and pale with hunger, and though he isn't saying anything, he's warning me to back away. To leave this place behind.

It's dark. The fire has dimmed. No, I correct myself. Tristan made it dim when he healed himself. When he hid his scars. He drew energy from the flames. That's why he was drawn to the fire. Not really for the warmth, but for the strength.

I look past him to the ashes and he follows my gaze. He looks back at me, as if for confirmation, before he grabs more wood and stokes the fire again. He is so simple, he probably thinks I am worried about the fire instead of my sanity.

The flames hiss and snap once more and it's a long time before either of us speaks again. Tristan seems content with the silence and I realize he's more than used to it. He wanders about the room. He makes the bed, cleans the dried blood from his face, uses his fingers to dust off the shelves of the book case. And all the while, I stare at the flames, mesmerized by their shifting shades. I realize that this isn't so bad.

What did I think I knew, anyway? I don't even know what fire is. No one does. All we know is that it's heat. But for some reason, I decided that was all I needed to know. Why had I set up that limitation like a barrier?

Life is full of barriers. We just ignore them because it's easier that way. Why are there so many different eye colors? Why do some of us like sour and some sweet? Why do I hear the dead? I turn my gaze to Tristan. I'm sure I look ridiculous with the expression on my face but he doesn't laugh at me. He looks down at me as he dusts off a book with his sleeve, his countenance simple but curious.

He can't think enough to understand my confusion. When you're half dead, you must experience the world differently. When Tristan is near the fire, I know he feels the heat but he also feels the strength, which I can't. I know I walk on the ground and that that's the way it is for everyone alive, but Tristan crawled on a wall. Maybe when we die, the barriers of understanding that we set up in life disappear.

I start to feel guilty as I notice the piece of fabric Tristan left on the hearth. Lace from my mother's wedding dress stained with blood.

Tristan may be simple, but that naiveté is the reason I'm still alive. He helped me for no reason other than I am human being. He fed me because I was hungry. Right now we are locked in a room, I am injured, and never once have I thought that he might try to force himself on me. I've never suspected it because though he has a body, he's never had the impulse.

That's why he's so attractive. It isn't just his looks. It's because I'm a Listener and he's half spirit. An innocence clings to him so intently that I can't help but be charmed by it. Now that I know the truth about him, I feel a desire to protect him. He could have easily turned into an angry, dangerous entity like the corpse, but he hasn't. He has chosen the difficult route of resistance.

I climb to my feet and cross over to him. He stops reading the titles on the spines of his books to look at me. He offers me a small smile, as if he can't read my face. Considering how many human customs he has forgotten, it's remarkable that he can communicate with me as well as he does.

I take his cool hand in mine and squeeze it. "I want to help you."

His smile fades. He shakes his head.

"This isn't right. Tristan, this isn't fair. I know she cared about you once, but she's no longer the person you knew. She must have been very selfish to have done this to you."

I wonder if she was his mother and thinks she's still lingering to protect her son, like Megan's grandma. He tugs his hand out of mine and crosses over to the other side of the room by the bed, as if he's trying to get away.

"She doesn't belong here," I continue. "Her spirit should be with the rest of the dead. We need to help her – or force her – to join them."

Tristan whips his head around to look at me. "Force her? No, no, no, no..." He begins pacing.

"Then abandon her. What would happen if I was to take you with me and we left this place behind?"

He stops his pacing and looks rather self-conscious.

"Tristan?"

"I don't always have a body." He is often cold, sure, but I just held his hand. It was solid. And he couldn't heal to the point of scarring if he didn't have a body. He cuts off my response, as if he knows what I'm thinking. "When I'm weak after she has fed on me, I don't have a body."

I blink at him. As hard as his mere existence is to grasp, my experiences in this house are starting to make more sense. It was his screaming that I head when I first entered the dwelling. "That's why I never saw you when I first searched the house..."

"I was here," he says quietly. "You just couldn't see me. And I was too weak to say hello."

I don't know why, but that makes me smile.

"She's unstoppable, and when she's angry, she..." He trails off. I want to know what he was going to say, but he looks pained enough as it is.

"She left me alone for hours," I say, "waiting for me to starve. That's when you recovered your strength."

Tristan nods and folds his arms over his chest as if he's cold. "She knew I helped you." His hugging of himself is growing neurotic as he grabs at his clothing. "She was upset. She uses the candles and lamps for her own energy yet snuffs them out when I dare." He's now grabbing at his vest and shirt. "If not for this fire, I would never have recovered enough." He looks like he must be hurting himself.

I cross over to Tristan and rest my hands on his to stop his fidgeting. "Is that why you were bleeding?" I ask as I gently pull his hands away from his torso.

He nods. "I wasn't whole. Old wounds..."

I reach up to brush his hair away from his temple and he flinches. There isn't any trace of a mark.

He crosses over to the fire. "She can summon me whenever she wants to. The only reason she hasn't yet is because she is sorting out what to do. Or trying to. She knows she can't get you in here. So she'll come after you again the moment you step out."

He looks around the room, as if realizing that it is there, and I wonder if he sometimes slips in and out of the spirit world, even while he has a body.

"Are you hungry? I should catch you more rats."

"Don't you need to eat as well?"

"Yes, though not as often as I did when I was alive. Not nearly as often."

I sit down on the bed. "That's why you took the dead animals from Sacrifice Rock."

"At first I thought it was hunters being generous with their catch. They kept leaving it out so I helped myself. In fact, I still have some smoked pork in the larder if you'd like some."

I haven't had pig in so long that I am already salivating. "I'd love some."

He grins. "Then I shall bring it to you." He steps over to the door.

"Wait," I say. He pauses. "The last time you went out, she hurt you."

Tristan looks confused. "Because she summoned me. She hasn't summoned me now."

"Let's stay here for a while. I still have a rat," I say.

I sit down on the hearth and stick the rat back into the fire, above the flames, to heat it up. Tristan sits next to me and places his folded hands between his knees. When the rat is warm, I tear off a leg and offer it to him who puts the whole thing in his mouth and swallows. Trying not to stare, I offer him the other leg but he waves it off.

"I am full, thank you."

He sighs contentedly as I eat the rest of the rat. And if I'm not mistaken, he looks rather proud.

"Isn't this wonderful?" he says. "You, me, the rat, the fire."

I laugh until I realize he's not joking. He doesn't seem to notice my slip.

"I didn't know what I was missing all this time. Of course, I knew it was something. But that something was so difficult to grasp that it evaded me for ages. It would have been easier were I not so forgetful. Which is probably why I couldn't remember what I wanted."

This is the most he has ever spoken about himself, and

unprompted, as well. I wonder if spending time with the living is restoring his mind.

"And what was that?" I ask, licking the grease off of my dirty fingers. I need to wash.

He grins. "A friend."

I can't help but grin back. A friend indeed. I start to feel guilty when I realize that he has been out here all of this time, so lonesome, while an entire village sits on the edge of his woods.

"If you could go as far as Sacrifice Rock, then why can't you come live in the village?" He has that self-conscious look on his face again. "When you have a body, I mean," I add.

His expression relaxes and his eyes look timid. He leans in towards my face but I don't back up. "May I?" he asks, even as his forehead presses against mine.

I don't have time to answer before I hear whispers in my mind.

"I'll show you." His breath puffs against my lips. The whispers grow louder and I realize they're his. That they were what I heard outside the forest and approaching the house. That he was the one asking for help all along. Not her.

The whispers weave around my mind like vines and then something happens to me that never has before. I live his memory.

Chapter Nine

I am Tristan. I am hiding in the house, in a corner by the fireplace. I am one with the darkness. I have no body. I feel the dull, exhausted ache that comes after the fade of intense pain. She has just fed on me. I am weak and can't move.

The candle flames around me begin jerking as if dancing a jig. I feel them changing. I know that means I am losing focus and losing time. Hours have passed suddenly. I feel better. Stronger. I drift out of my hiding place and through the door. I think it was the door. I can't see it. But I know it's there.

It's thrilling to glide. I feel like the bottom of my stomach is perpetually falling out, giving me shivers inside. But then my gliding slows to jerking. Jerking to thumping. I can hear footsteps. My footsteps. My body is returning. I am walking.

I can feel the cold. I look down at my hands. White-hot pain sears my arms where my scars are. I don't have the strength to fight it. Not right now. So I accept it and let my scars remain. My sleeves hurt them. I roll back the fabric. They feel a little better now.

The woods are dark, but I still have my spirit senses. I don't need to see where each tree is to know it's there. It is a rare cloudless night. I stop in a clearing. I can see the moon and stars. I am filled with wonder. From the tips of my fingers to the depths of my heart. It consumes my mind and senses. I lie down.

I gaze up at the crescent moon, attended by stars. Time passes. It is just the grass and the wind and the heavens. Just the joys of being alive. I can't remember anything before this moment. There is only the moon and the outside. Clouds stream in and veil the sky. I wake up. Am I a tree? Am I grass? I move. No, I am man and the moon is gone. I am disappointed. So disappointed that I sulk for some time. Until my clothes are damp with dew. Then I am restless. I get up and start walking. I don't know where I am going until I see the lights in the distance. The village.

I approach quietly, resting my cheek on the bark of a cedar. I can see nearly a hundred houses. They glitter like little flames. Warmth and family. I want to be in one of those little homes. I want to feel the fire. Smell the soup. Hear the baby trying to talk. I want to see happy faces. Where did my happy face go? Someone used to smile at me. Who was she?

Wait, what am I doing here? Where am I?

A door closes. I see a young lady. She has a scarf on her head. The hair underneath is yellow. She is shaking out a blanket. I can't look away. She is alive and young. She is bones and rushing blood. She is warm. I step towards her. Step. Yes, I have legs. I am a man. Now I remember.

She folds the blanket up. I want something. I feel cold and hollow like a jack-o-lantern. Because I want. I want. I want her... to feel me. So badly. Because unlike the others, I can feel her. Warm strength like fire. She slows in her work. I know she can sense me. She can help me with the emptiness within. She can hear me calling to her.

I lift my foot to take another step. I hear a voice behind me. It is a man. I dart back behind the cedar. I notice the light from a lantern in the woods, several yards away. Then another light. Hunters. I look back to the girl, but she has gone inside. The hollowness is now a hole. I am alone. No one listens. No one listens.

The hunters are my friends. They take care of me. They leave me food. They are kind men. I slip through the forest towards their lights. I don't make a sound. I am good at being quiet. Is that what I am? Am I quietness?

One of the hunters is a young man. His hair tied back. He is behind the others. Three men are with him. One is sitting on the stump of a felled tree. He is examining his boot. The other two lean against trunks, waiting. They have a dead rabbit, but that is all. I pause a few yards away and peer at them from behind a tree. The youngest is the boy with the hair tied back. He is the only one listening to the woods around them.

I watch. He slowly turns his head and looks at me. I smile. He has seen me. But it must be too dark for he doesn't react. He didn't see me after all. One of the other men speaks to him.

"Draven, rabbit's yours."

The boy shakes his head.

"Don't play games," the man says. "We've got a system. It's your turn."

I step closer. Games? Games with a dead rabbit? I've never heard of this game. I can't remember any games, though. I don't know any games. Maybe the hunters can teach me.

The man on the stump sighs. "My boot's worn clear through."

"Hello," I say but none of them seem to hear me. I try again, louder this time. "Hello."

"My brother left me a pair that might fit you," one of the men continues.

Why can't they hear me? The boy they called Draven is looking my way again. His eyes are so dark they seem like they are made of night. I tilt my head to the side and wonder if he sees me. He steps over to the others. "We need to move," he says.

The three men pivot to look at him. They rely on his senses more than their own. One withdraws a knife. Draven's eyes flick in my direction. The others tense.

Oh dear. They know I am here but are afraid. I must try harder.

"Hello," I say again, as loud as I can.

"Something's watching us, all right," one of the men says, readying his crossbow.

"You think it's the beast?"

"Could be."

Beast? What beast? There's a beast in these woods?

I run towards the men, towards the safety of their lanterns. I am not careful. I snuff out one of their lights. I didn't mean to. One of the men shouts. They aim their weapons at the woods. I step up behind one.

"I'm sorry," I say. He stares ahead and starts to move in towards the others. I rest a hand on his shoulder and am about to apologize again when he screams.

I let go. He jerks away. The others point their weapons at me. I am frightened. So frightened that I can't move.

"Something grabbed me!" the man shouts.

"What was it?"

"It was me," I shout. They can't hear me. I step towards the lamplight. I reach out my hands to show I have no weapons. I can see my scars in the golden light.

They see me now. But only the ugly part of me. They shout and one throws a knife. I leap into the air and latch onto a tree trunk. An arrow whizzes past my head. Is this the dead rabbit game?

I don't like it. They are screaming to kill me. I scurry up further. Fire burns in my shoulder. I am paralyzed. The boy with the crossbow shot me. He hurt me.

I am sad. So sad that I shake. He hurt me. The men all want to hurt me. They are not my friends after all.

"Did you get him?" one asks.

Mean men. Mean. Mean. Mean.

I scream. My shoulder hurts. It hurts so much that my strength is fading. I draw energy from their lantern. It snuffs out, leaving them in darkness. It isn't enough. I can't hold onto my body any more. I scream again as I fall. I never hit the ground. I have no body.

I zip through the forest. I huddle in the corner by the fireplace. The hunters hurt me. Why would they hurt me? They weren't my friends. I am empty and cold. Cold. Hollow.

Then she fills me. I can do nothing to push her out. She is amused by me. *You will never be one of them,* she coos. *You are mine, darling. Stay where you are safe...*

Safe, yes, I am safe here. Nothing can harm me. Except for her. Then she feeds. I hardly have anything left to give. But still she takes. Until all I am is quietness.

Tristan pulls his forehead away from mine. Suddenly I am back in my body. My beautifully warm, solid body. I will never take it for granted again.

The dejection, that terrible despair that consumed me is gone. Tristan is looking at his hands, appearing smaller than he is. Red has blossomed on his shoulder, staining the white of his shirt, as if the memory made his wound fresh again. I don't realize I have tears on my cheeks until they start to dry.

The happy emotions Tristan felt were so consuming, so intoxicatingly pleasant that I long to feel them again. Why can't the living feel such passion? Yet the depth of his woe and hurt were just as strong. Even after Scarlet's death, I have never felt so vulnerable within myself. So deeply shamed and unloved. So trapped. Yet that is Tristan's existence.

I wipe my cheeks. Draven never knew his bolt had hit its mark. And the girl with the scarf on her head, shaking out the blanket...

"Did you know that was me you saw?"

He nods. "You're the only living person I've ever felt."

"Felt?"

"Your light." He smiles faintly as he looks to me. "We are like moths. We know you will listen."

I have often wondered what I feel like to the dead. How they know I am a Listener. I barely recall the day Tristan saw me. I often hear stray whispers here and there. Bits and pieces that I can't make sense of, so I ignore. This was probably one of those moments. Then I remind myself of what I learned before I slipped into his memory. If I can't find a way to help him, no one will.

And if there is one thing I gained from his memory, it's that the corpse doesn't have as strong a hold on him as he thinks. She feeds on him until he is almost nothing, yes. But she needs him and he doesn't need her.

Gloom is still bowing his spine. The memory is too fresh. "The hunters didn't understand you. They acted in fear."

Tristan holds a hand to his shoulder, wincing.

"And this spirit woman, this corpse, she is doing the same thing. She's not the one with the power. You are."

He considers this for a moment. "I can't stop her from feeding on me."

"But you're getting so much better. The more time I spend with you, the more human you seem."

He smiles faintly.

"It's doing you good. And the stronger you are, the less she'll be able to hurt you. So let's focus on ways you gain strength."

Tristan crosses to the fire. It dims as the wound on his shoulder fades. "I can use fire to heal."

I smile. "Good. What else?"

"Um..." He looks around the room for inspiration. "Speaking with you helps my thoughts stay straight. That is a good thing."

"It is."

He paces as he thinks, his step quick and light and off the wall whenever he reaches one, reminding me that he has a ways to go. "The more I remember of life, the more... stable I feel. Like I belonged here once and might again."

Drawing strength from fire is sticking in my head. "How can you feed off flames?"

"They're a link to the Netherworld." He stops pacing. "At least, that's how I see it."

I'm about to say that doesn't make sense when I realize that it does. I've always felt kinship with fire. The flames warm my body and cook my food. They give me life and survival. Watching their shifting shades relaxes me and I feel like there has always been fire as long as there have been people. Like fire is so important to us that it's emblazoned in our spirits.

Out of control, it is utterly destructive. It kills in seconds. It destroys lives. Yet in its wake is rebirth. Green shoots always stir from the ashes. It is a giver and a taker. A creator and a destroyer. And that amazing force that we experience as fire is experienced as another form of energy in the Netherworld. In the realm of the dead that isn't a place, but a state of being. Fire is with us, even after we die, which would explain our primal connection with it. Our need to bring it into our homes.

And then I am thinking of the burning circle and grow cold. The sun is heat and fire. The corpse devours any light she can.

"Tristan," I gasp. "It's her. She's the cause of all of this. She has devoured so much light that she has created a hole. A void in the spirit world. She should be there but she's not, she's here."

He is studying me with large eyes and I know he is keeping up with me.

"She has caused a rift. She's the source of the darkness."

Chapter Ten

Tristan falls to his knees. "No," he whispers, as if the weight of being connected to such an individual is overwhelming.

My shock evaporates in the heat of my anger. Not only has she caused the darkness that killed the men who were sent for help, but also another.

"Elias thought she was a witch..." I whisper, my chest clenching.

"Who?" Tristan squeaks.

"He blamed her for the darkness and burnt her at the stake, but it didn't change anything."

Hunger grew. Women became barren. I stopped bleeding each month. Then starvation claimed its first victim: the blacksmith's apprentice. If the burly young man had starved to death, then the rest of us would soon follow. Fear spread like wildfire. And one by one, the families of my village consented to the sacrifice. It was all we had left. I wouldn't be here, broken and bleeding, if it wasn't for the Bringer's selfishness.

I kneel before Tristan. When he doesn't look at me, I place a hand on either of his shoulders. When he still won't look at me, I cup his chin in my hand. Our eyes meet and my voice is firm. This is no longer just a battle for his liberty.

"Tristan, I am going to free you and defeat her."

There's a bang down the hall. Something must have fallen. Tristan's eyes are timid. "You want me to pretend I'm human?"

"As human as possible." There's another bang, closer this time. They're footsteps. Heavy, heavy footsteps. The lamps in the hall are suddenly all lit. The hair on the back of my neck stands on end.

She is coming. His eyes widen as he realizes it at the same time I do.

"Focus on life. On being alive."

Bang. He winces as another footstep falls. "She is summoning me."

I slip my fingers into his and squeeze his hand. "Feel how warm I am."

"It's going to hurt." He looks at our hands with dejection. *Bang*!

"Tristan," I rest my hand on his cheek and am surprised by how soft it is. "Look at me." He does. "Tell me who you were in life."

"I don't remember."

"Yes, you do. Your name was Tristan. It came to me because I already knew it from your whispers. Tristan. You lived in this house. You must have had a lot of money to have such a fine home."

Bang.

His eyes narrow slightly. "Yes..." He looks around the room with renewed interest. "Money... coins... gold... my father had gold. Then I had gold."

Bang. She is only yards away.

He rises and I keep my hand joined to his, trying to anchor him. He crosses over to the desk and runs his hand over the surface. "I used to write at this spot."

"What did you write?" *Bang*. I squeeze his hand.

"I... I kept a ledger... no. A journal." He lets go of my hand just as the footsteps stop. She is outside the door. Tristan lifts the top of the desk and pulls out a leather bound book. He uses his sleeve to wipe away the dust. Then he goes unnaturally stiff and drops the journal.

I grab onto his shoulder. "Fight her, Tristan. Tell me what you wrote in the book."

"Nothing."

"Your name is Tristan. You live in this house."

He is looking at me with the most horribly blank eyes.

"You kept a journal."

He blinks, his face empty, then shoves my hand off his shoulder and moves like a puppet, heading for the exit.

I run to the door and press my back against it, blocking it. I don't care that there's only a piece of wood separating me from the corpse that wants to kill me. My chest is heavy. I'm hungry, I'm tired, my ankle is getting better, and I'm sick of being afraid of her.

"Leave him," I mutter, my voice deeper than I've ever heard it before. "Now."

The door hammers in response, jarring my bones. I wince as it smacks the back of my head, but I don't budge. Tristan is standing before me, as if waiting for a command.

I look him in the eye. "You are kind and gentle, Tristan. You have every reason not to be, but you're a good person. Which means you're strong."

I reach out and take his hand in mine again. At our touch, he blinks and looks from our linked hands to my face with a small smile.

"Hello," he says, as if we've just met.

I shake my head. "You know me. I'm Willow." I squeeze his hand.

"Willow..." he whispers. His expression turns pensive. Recognition dawns in his eyes but then he jerks and falls onto his back. For a second, he looks like he is a fish out of water, gasping for air. Then he lets out the most terrible scream.

I wheel about to pound on the door. "I said leave him," I shout.

Tristan's scream peters out and he drags himself across the room and up the wall, whimpering. I want to go to him but there's nothing I can do to comfort him.

"Leave him!"

Tristan screams again and I think his throat must be in shreds. There's no other way he could be making those agonizing sounds. Blood is rushing from the wound on the side of his face which has opened up again. He falls from the wall with a thud then spasms. More screams.

His pain is like a presence in the room. I have to stop it. I twist the key and yank open the door, ready to punch and claw, to shove and tear. But there's nothing there. Tristan's screaming stops, as well. I look behind me and he's gone. The room is empty.

What just happened? It sounds like something is sliding around downstairs. Another set of lamps and candles flicker to life below me. I peer over the railing and it takes a moment for my eyes to adjust. Then I see it.

Tristan is lying in a heap, unconscious. Something invisible is dragging him into the dining room.

I run down the first few steps then grab onto the railing to stop myself. This is a trap.

As a spirit, even as a corpse, there is little she can directly do to harm me. But there is plenty she can do to fool me into harming myself. My knuckles are white against the banister. I want so badly to go down there and attack her. But even if I had a knife, what good would a weapon be against a dead body? I might chop off her head, sure, but so long as she has Tristan to feed from, she will find a way to reattach it.

So I wait near the top of the stair. I listen with my physical senses. I hear nothing. Just the creak of the house settling. Maybe she's gone.

I can still see Tristan's shoe sticking out from around the corner. I slowly descend the stairs, step by step. She scared me into running down them and hurting myself once. I won't make the same mistake again. Nearing the landing, I lean, trying to peer around the corner into the dining room to see what state Tristan is in. He isn't there. My eyes dart to where I'd seen his shoe. It's gone.

She's playing games with me.

Tristan had said that she was trying to figure out how to deal with me. How to kill me. I see now that Tristan is critical to both of our plans. As much as I use him to try to weaken her, she'll use him to try to manipulate me. I don't like it. Not at all. He doesn't deserve to be treated like a pawn. Like a plaything.

I square my shoulders and walk into the dining room. The lamps and candles all snuff out as soon as I do so. I pause for a moment, the hair on the back of my neck and arms standing on end. That's how I know she's still here. Good. I want her to witness what I'm about to do.

I walk into the parlor that is musty with mildewing furniture. I can't see but I've gotten used to judging my surroundings in the dark. To feeling for things. I pat around the mossy hearth for a few moments then find what I'm looking for. Flint and steel. Crouching before the fireplace, I strike the steel against the flint, making a spark. The brief surge of light illuminates dried leaves filling the fireplace. I don't have any tinder so it takes a few tries, but the leaves start to smolder then catch fire. The combustion surges up the chimney and the room is so bright that I shield my eyes.

After gathering some kindling from a stack beside the cook fire in the kitchen, I stoke the flames. After some coaxing, I have a roaring fire blazing in the hearth and the moss growing around it begins to steam. I warm my hands and am about to sit on the hearth when I see the upholstered chairs facing it. I'm sure she sat in one of these chairs in life.

I scoot one towards the flames and sink into it. It stinks and is damp and half the cushioning on the bottom has been stolen by mice. But I don't mind. I'm not doing this for the comfort. I'm doing it to make myself at home in her house.

A draft picks up, as if I've left a window open, but I haven't. The flames flicker from the weak breeze. It might be enough to snuff out a candle or lamp, but not a fire like this. I smile. *Not so powerful now, are you?*

After a while, the breeze stops, but I know she hasn't given up. I remain in my chair, even though it's making my dress damp. I wonder where Tristan is. He doesn't have a body right now, that much I know. I would quiet my mind to try to listen for him, but that would be too risky with her still around. I'm not sure what she could do to me as a Listener, but my instincts tell me not to invite her in again.

I'm hungry and very thirsty. Tristan brought me water from somewhere, so they must have access within the house. I get up and grab one of the thinner burning logs and carry it as a torch. She doesn't snuff it out right away, which makes me think she's observing me. Calculating. I carry my fire into the kitchen and light a few candles there.

A hand pump is in the corner. My father bought one once from a traveling merchant. He tried to sell it in our village but no one would buy it. They all laughed at such a contraption since the well worked good enough, and the blacksmith eventually bought it for the metal. I pump enough water to fill the basin and drink and drink. When I can't hold anymore, I fill the basin again and wash.

Though I know Tristan and the woman are still present somewhere, I'm not shy enough to keep my dress on. I slip out of it and wash my body and can feel my hips sticking out of my abdomen. I'm thinner than I was when I left home. Shivering for a few minutes, I drip dry, then pull my mother's wedding dress back on. It takes a while to tug it up over my damp skin, then I head back over to the fire and warm up. It feels so good to be clean and watered. My energy is renewed.

I comb my fingers through my hair and realize I still have some of the dried pea flowers my mother had stuck in on the day of the sacrifice. I carefully pull them out and gather the frail blossoms in my lap. Combing my hair out with my fingers, I arrange it to cover the bare portion of my back, helping me stay warm. After a while, I light more candles in the room. When she doesn't snuff them out, I light every lamp and candle I find. They never seem to burn down.

The house is now so illuminated that I can see every cobweb billowing in the corners, every pile of droppings. A door closes upstairs. I know it isn't Tristan. He wouldn't make noises to try to peak my curiosity. It's her, trying to draw me away. I'm not taking the bait. The door opens and closes again.

The first time I heard her feed on Tristan, he had been in pain before I even noticed her footsteps. This time, she couldn't touch him until she was outside the door. Anchoring him to the world of the living had been working. I see now my best chance of defeating her. I must flaunt life in her face.

Chapter Eleven

I start by hunting downstairs for anything useful. I find the linen closet. Anything on top, exposed to air, has mold on it. But there are several clean tablecloths in the middle of the stack. I take one of the molding ones and get it wet. For the next several hours, I dust the house. The cloth is soon so covered in spider webs clumping the dust that I have to wash it out again. Then again. Over and over, I wring out the rag. I wash the windows and the sills. The table and chairs. The kitchen. Then I find a broom and sweep up all of the rat droppings and fallen leaves. I pry the moss off the hearth.

By the time I am done, I am exhausted and need to wash again. My ankle is throbbing once more. I rest for a little while, but since Tristan isn't back yet, I keep going. I light the lamps upstairs and clean. There isn't much tidying up to do in my and Tristan's room, but I do it all the same. I leave the other two rooms alone. They're not worth the effort.

I face the door at the end of the hall. I know what happened last time I touched it. Steeling myself, I march towards it. I know what I'm doing must be upsetting her, for I'm taking over her house and claiming it as my own.

This ought to put the final nail in the coffin. Using my cloth, I wash the chains and lock holding her door shut. To my surprise, she doesn't react, so I work at the chains until they are shining metal once more.

After sweeping up the floors in the hall, I head back down and stoke the fire again. Finally finished, I wash my face and arms then sit by the hearth. Lighted and cleaned, the rooms actually look inviting. The walls are still mildewing and their paper is peeling, but it seems livable now. At least more than it was.

I lean my head back against the armchair, closing my eyes, letting my body relax. The fire has dried the upholstery out a bit. It still smells of must but it feels so nice to sit. I wonder what my family is doing at home right now. Do they think I'm dead?

Poor Jasper. He has lost another sister. He didn't understand what death was until Scarlet died. Though neither did I, ironically enough. Hearing the dead and losing someone are two completely different things.

At first I couldn't believe that she was gone. I thought it must have been a mistake. Another girl with raven hair. Someone else's big sister, not mine. Then I felt like I couldn't breathe. Like I'd never be able to breathe with ease again. It was her. She was dead. She was gone. She had passed through the veil. She was now one of those simple, eerily confused whispers I heard. She couldn't hug me anymore. She couldn't warm our bed or braid my hair or tell me stories.

I fled into the woods. I had heard whispers there before, whispers I now know belonged to Tristan. I wept and wept and when I finally stopped, I closed my eyes and listened. I made my mind a calm surface and felt for the slightest ripple. I wanted to feel her presence, but there was nothing. It wasn't fair. I was burdened by the secrets of the dead, by the hopes and failures of strangers, yet couldn't hear my own sister.

I wasn't far into the forest so the lights from the cabins of Morrot were still visible. I could see enough to spot pinecones and rocks to hurl. And hurl them I did. When I had exhausted the debris nearby, I hugged my shawl around me in the cold.

Wings fluttered near enough to fan me but I was too worn out to react. Draven appeared at my side, Lady on his shoulder. He sat down in front of me, cross-legged. He had his crossbow but was empty-handed, except for Lady. Her black-capped head and white speckled chest were beautiful, and with her large brown eyes, she looked rather like her master. In fact, the way the two were peering at me with their heads slightly cocked, they looked like twins. I wondered who imitated whom.

"No," I said.

Draven just sat there silent.

"No," I repeated. I didn't want to talk about Scarlet. I had reached the place where my tears were temporarily exhausted. Where I was so tired inside that I was numb. I knew that as soon as I regained my strength, the pain would return. I wasn't ready for that.

Lady nuzzled Draven's hair. Her talons were shredding the shoulder of his tunic and the skin beneath was red. I realized he wasn't wearing his wrist guard, either. His arm was bleeding from her claws. He followed my gaze then sighed, moving Lady to his arm so that he could look at her.

"She's weak. She won't live much longer. I want to feel her whenever I can."

He kissed the top of the falcon's head. She flapped her wings, stretching them, her claws digging into his arm, squeezing out new blood, but Draven didn't flinch. I realized then that Lady was more than a friend and a hunting partner. She was a link to his father.

Though I hated the idea of anyone claiming to know how I felt, I knew that Draven understood. Like Lucian, we didn't have any warning before Scarlet's death.

I sniffled and wished that Lady wouldn't die. That none of us had to die. Scarlet had once said that she was comforted to know the Netherworld was real and not just a story. I wasn't comforted. I wanted my sister, not a simpleton spirit. I hated to think that was what she had become. She was so vibrant and full of ideas.

"Does it get any easier?" I whispered.

"This has changed you. There is no going back."

I wiped at my cheeks, even though I knew my tears had dried.

"I don't think I can do this."

He studied me for a while, and I knew he was remembering the first few days after his father died. Then he shifted Lady to his shoulder and reached out for me. I took his hand and he tugged me to him. His other slid on my shoulder and guided me down until I was resting against him. He was warm and whole. I snaked an arm around his waist and was happy that I could still feel muscle on his torso. He wasn't wasting away like some of the other boys.

I rested my head on his thigh and his hand was warm on my shoulder. I know he must've felt like it was impossible, too, but here he was, at my side. Solid. He had lived through his grief. He was still living through his grief. Some of my hair was sticking to the dried tears on my cheeks so he brushed it away then combed his fingers through my curls.

The cold, the uneven ground and pine needles beneath me became comfortable in that moment. Then Draven did something I had never heard him do before. He hummed.

At first I thought it was a lullaby, but then I realized it was Midsummer's Song.

Whether in this life or the next,
Even after sunset in the west
The light will return from high above
For it is my heart and you are my love

Lady ruffled her feathers and the sounds of her fidgeting and the scent of leather and pine staining Draven were so familiar that I could've fallen asleep. He focused on one section of my hair for some time, and I belatedly realized he was braiding it. I lay like that for a long while. Long past when the comfort faded.

I eventually heard my mother's panicked voice calling for me. She had just lost one daughter. Now she was looking for the second.

Sighing, I stirred and sat up. My legs had fallen asleep and I had to wait for them to tingle back to life. My hand was still resting on

Draven's hip. He pulled my curls forward and arranged my hair, positioning his braid at the front. Then he took my shawl and draped it over my head, tying it at my chin.

Linking his hand with mine at his hip, he helped me to my feet. We walked back to the village and I hugged on to his arm and leaned against him for warmth. I didn't have the heart to say goodbye at my door, even if I'd see him the next day. So I slipped back inside without a word.

My mother had hugged me tightly. Then she fingered my braid.

"That's pretty," she said. I reached up to feel it as I sat on my bed. My fingers slipped over the thin bumps of his weaving, then over something soft and thin. A feather. It was one of Lady's.

I thought of Draven differently after that day. I didn't want to, but I did. Growing up with him like a cousin made it difficult to think of him as anything else. But when I kept the braid for days because it was his hands that had made it, I knew he was right. I had changed. There was no going back.

The fire pops, startling me. I'm tired of being alone. At the very least, being with Draven after my sister's death, feeling his hands on my body, sparked something inside. It reminded me of how much there was to enjoy in life, how much potential we have if we can only live. How much beauty there is in adoring another.

I sigh. I think I've been sleeping. The fire has burnt low and my neck is aching from the angle I've been slumped in. I wonder how much time has passed since I cleaned her door. Time in which she hasn't reacted. I hear a scuff behind me and turn to spot Tristan.

He is whole again and peering at me with deer-like eyes. I'm afraid to make any sudden movements lest I startle him.

"Hello," I say, greeting him as he has so often greeted me.

He smiles then runs his hand over the other armchair as he approaches, his body language shy. "I like what you've done," he says.

"I did it for you."

He's twisting up the bottom of his vest, and I realize that he's flattered I would put out such effort for him.

I smile and pat the cushion of the other armchair. He returns my smile and takes a seat.

"How do you feel?" I ask.

"Wonderful."

"It sounded like she hurt you badly."

Tristan slowly slumps in his chair until the seat of his pants is half off, as if trying to hide from her. He doesn't make any other response so I work with what I have.

"Comfortable?"

"Quite."

To each his own. We sit like this for some time. Me curled up, him slumped in a position that doesn't look the least relaxing. I give him several minutes of peace before I say what I must. "She's going to use you, you know. To get to me."

He sighs. "I know."

"That means she'll hurt you again."

"She'll hurt me anyway so it doesn't make much difference." He slowly looks to me, his black bangs in his eyes. "She doesn't like me making friends with you. She doesn't like me remembering life."

"Wait..." I shift my position to better peer at him. "We keep talking about you as if you're dead. Do you remember dying?"

He shakes his head no. "But I am forgetful."

"I don't think that's something you'd be able to forget."

Tristan looks down at his hands as he toys with the end of his vest again. I realize he's missing a button. "It's rather unfair," he says. "I shouldn't have to be this way if I never actually died."

He's right. I don't even understand how it's possible for him to exist as both a spirit and a body. He's more than a body, though. He has a mind of his own. He's a person. "I want you to live as much like me as you can."

He looks me up and down. "I'm not sure your dress would suit me."

I stare at him for a moment before I laugh. The sly smile on his face tells me that this wasn't a slip up in etiquette. He was making a joke. He is definitely more human.

"Do you still have the smoked pork?" I ask.

"Yes."

"Then let's eat it. Only not in the room. Let's eat it properly, in the dining room."

Tristan sits up in his chair. "A dinner party?"

I don't know what that is but I nod my head.

"Excellent!" He leaps up and claps his hands. "You must forgive me for not having thought of this sooner." He smacks his forehead. "Stupid mind, rolling around all the time."

"It's all right," I say, trying to interrupt his abuse. "I wasn't suitable for it earlier. But I've washed now."

As I rise, he eyes my tattered gown then shoots me the most mischievous look I've ever seen him wear. I am suddenly once more aware that I am in the presence of a handsome young man who is more than just a lonesome spirit. "I think I have something that shall suit the occasion."

Chapter Twelve

An hour later, we are seated at the dinner table in the dining room. The white tablecloth has done wonders to spruce up the space. Tristan has pulled out several candelabras and their flickering lights cheerily illuminate the table. Goblets glisten with water and I've placed the dried pea blossoms from my hair in the center as decorations. A large piece of smoked pork rests on my plate and a significantly smaller portion is on Tristan's. He has put on a black jacket, a bow around his collar, and has slicked back his hair with a wet comb. Though no matter how hard he tried, stray hairs have escaped to frame his face.

I have stuck up my curls with a few hairpins I found in a drawer, and I feel extravagant in my gown. I don't know where he got it from, but Tristan presented me with the most beautiful dress I have ever seen. Its fabric is a deep, burgundy red that appears to have shadows when it catches the light. It is covered in little black beads stitched into patterns of swirling roses. It's a little long and the shoulders are a little too wide, so I am wearing the sleeves on my biceps, like I did with my mother's dress.

I feel like a girl in one of Scarlet's stories.

Tristan holds up his napkin to show me what to do with it. He unfolds it and places it on his lap, and I do the same. He has such an impish expression on his face that I can't stop smiling. Picking up our knives and forks, we each survey our meals. My piece of meat is so big that I am tempted to save it to bring home to my family. But I am so hungry and this food will give me the strength to ensure that they have much more meat in the years to come.

He holds up his fork in his left hand and sticks it into his meat then saws off a small bite with the knife in his right. Placing the bite in his mouth, he never switches hands, and I have to focus to mimic him. I've never paid any attention to the way I eat. No one in my village does. We use our hands half the time.

As Tristan takes another refined bite, I chuckle. "Where did you learn to eat like that?"

"My mother," he says then ungracefully shoves the rest of the meat into his mouth and swallows it whole, making me giggle again. "Manners were very important to her."

I'm grinning. "Tristan, you remember your mother. That's wonderful."

He arches a brow. "Wonderful? The woman was more focused on etiquette than affection. She'd slap the table whenever I didn't eat properly."

"I can only imagine what she'd think of you now."

He stares at me for a moment then barks out in laughter. It's the first time I've ever heard him make the sound and it is so sudden that I jump a little. Which makes me laugh.

The fires are roaring, the hearths all aglow. Tristan's understanding is growing in leaps and bounds. I can't think of anything more powerful against the Bringer than filling the house with laughter, so I let mine come freely.

Taking another bite, I try to mimic Tristan's manners then give up and eat the way I am used to. "Where are you from that has such customs?" I ask after I swallow.

"Southeast," he says. "A city, not a village. There are homes like this on every street. Well, not quite like this, but more like this than the houses in your village."

Though I try, I can't imagine what such a lavish place must look like. I didn't even know one existed. But my wonder at the image fades as the idea of so many fine homes makes me feel sick inside. Like they've forgotten something important and are unhappy. I like our little home where we feel the seasons, not that we have seasons anymore. "Why did you move here?"

He furrows his brow, focusing. "It had something to do with trade... I wanted to bring something..."

Even before the darkness, Morrot had very little contact with other villages. In part because we're so high in the mountains, but also because we were self-sufficient. We didn't need to trade.

My father is a merchant and if he has never met Tristan, then I wonder when Tristan first arrived here. He isn't old enough to have been here long, but then again, he has been trapped in-between. For all I know, he could be one hundred. But the house doesn't look decrepit enough to have survived a century.

"Medicine," he says. The line between his brows is deeper than I've ever seen it as he focuses. "I was trying to trade medicine for something. That was it. I wanted..." He looks up at me, the concentration gone as it becomes clear in his mind. "I wanted to help someone. We were going to live in the woods, away from those who thought ill of us. But then I wanted to stay. To bring your people medicine."

I study Tristan for a long while. He keeps trying to tuck his stray strands of hair away, but I like them there. It is little imperfections like that which make a person beautiful. He is beautiful.

While it would be hard for many to believe a wealthy man would be so generous, I know he is telling the truth. When we die, we become the most important parts of ourselves. Tristan has shown me such kindness and generosity as a half-spirit that I know such traits were integral to who he was in life. *Who he is*, I correct myself.

My cheeks flush a little when I realize I'm staring, but he doesn't seem to mind. He might not have noticed my reaction in the past, but I know he's capable of understanding it now. He looks down at his empty plate and bites his lip. "Guess it's rats from now on."

I smile. I wind up only eating half the pork for fear it'll make me sick to eat so much at once. The rest will make another meal.

The corpse has yet to make a move. For a brief moment, I wonder if I'm winning. But then I remind myself of what she did to Tristan earlier. It's not over yet. "What else happens at dinner parties?" I ask.

He raises his brows as he thinks, dabbing the corners of his mouth with his napkin. "Well, we've already eaten. We've conversed. That leaves only one thing."

"What's that?"

Tristan scoots his chair back and strides over to me. Tucking his left hand behind his back, he bows and holds out his right. "May I have this dance?"

I laugh and feel like I'm going to blush again but I don't. I rest my hand in his and hold up the hem of my dress as I rise, and he escorts me to the parlor where there is more floor space.

"What could be more living than a dance?" he whispers, resting a hand on my waist and twining his other in mine, and his skin and is warmer than before. There is a subtlety to the glint in his eyes. He's thinking more than one thing at a time. The problem now is that I don't know what. But I'll take the trade off if it means victory.

Tristan takes a step back, and I follow. Then one to the side, forward, and to the other side. At first I have to watch our feet to make sure I'm not stepping on his toes. I see how grimy my slippers have become and toss them aside. Barefoot, I can feel the smooth surface of the boards as they shift and creak beneath us. We repeat the moves and I realize we're performing a box step.

"One, two, three," he counts as we pick up the pace. I match his step easily enough, my elbow tucked in against his. I love to dance. We haven't danced in years. "One, two, three. One, two, three."

He lets go of my waist and extends his arm and I twirl. The dress is heavy with beads yet still it spins. I feel the hem wrap around my legs as I face him once more.

"Excellent! One, two, three," he continues, grinning.

I laugh. There is no subtlety here. No nuance. Just happiness. *One, two, three. One, two, three.* We dance in a square, I twirl. *One, two, three.*

"Music," I say. "We need music!"
Tristan sings.

"If I were a fish and you were the sea
I'd dance on your waves and bonny we'd be.
If you were a leaf and I were a tree
I'd catch you when you'd fall from me."

One, two, three. We're dancing so fast that I'm messing up the steps and laughing. I abandon my efforts and take the lead. I dance us in a circle, our hands on each other's waists.

"But you are the wolf and I am the moon
And it's your howl that is my boon.
I am the song and you are the dance
We may be different but I'll take the chance."

I'm almost tripping and Tristan is laughing as he sings. We weave around the chairs and low table. I smack into one and almost fall over.

"For without you I'm a flower gone dry,
A ship without sails,
A star without a sky."

I do trip this time and would've fallen over had Tristan not been holding onto me. I'm actually sweating a little, and lifting up the hem of the dress, I slump onto the upholstered seat wide enough for two. I fan my face, giggling.

"Willow, I must say," Tristan says as he catches his breath. "Your grace is beyond me."

That makes me laugh and incline my head in a pretend bow. "That's a beautiful song." Tristan plops onto the empty cushion beside me, his body radiating heat. "I haven't heard it before."

"You wouldn't have," he says. He's still trying to swipe his hair back. "In fact, you're wearing the dress of the woman who used to sing it."

My smile slips off my face. His family died. It's not like it's a surprise that I'm in a dead woman's gown. But Tristan has a strange look on his face. He starts laughing, almost maniacally.

"In fact," he pants. "It's rather funny." Though he's laughing, his eyes are wounded. "The woman who sang that song is the one we're trying to destroy. Can you believe it?"

He's listing to the side, as if he's literally off-balance. I feel sick to my stomach and it's not from the pork.

"She's my wife," Tristan gets out with a choke. I'm distracted from what he said because I'm worried he's being attacked again. But as he falls onto his hands and knees on the floor, I realize he's crying. "My own wife. She has trapped me. She hurts me. And I love her."

Chapter Thirteen

Tristan's back shakes as he weeps. I remain seated on the couch, sweat cooling against my skin. His wife. The corpse is his wife.

The pork now feels like it's rotting in my stomach. The idea of treating a loved one the way she treats Tristan is so unsettling that I'm having trouble keeping track of my thoughts. For some reason, I'm irritated that he didn't tell me who she was sooner. Surely he must've remembered when he gave me her gown. Then again, I experienced firsthand how full of holes his memory is, and it's none of my business that he was married once.

He has collapsed on the floor now, sobbing into the crook of his arm. I have no words to comfort him. No insight into how such a horrible truth could be possible. So instead, I do what Draven did for me.

Gathering up the dress, I kneel beside Tristan. I rest my hand on his back to let him know I'm there, then I run my fingers through his hair. It's so soft and he isn't warm anymore. In fact, he's shockingly cold. Like his sorrow is tugging him back into the spirit world.

I need to pull him out of this. Not just for the sake of destroying his wife, but because it's getting harder and harder to bear the sight of his suffering. I don't know if he even notices my touch, for he continues crying for some time. It's good for the human side of him to grieve, but I'm wary he'll trap himself in his sorrow.

"Tristan," I say softly. "You know that's not really her anymore." I don't tell him that spirits are intensified personalities of the living. "No one who loves you would hurt you like that."

He rolls over onto his back and looks up at me through a mess of hair and tear-stained cheeks. "She does it because she loves me."

His eyes have faded back to their simpler expression of hurt. I try to shove aside the thought that we're undoing all of the progress we've made.

"We wanted to be together. Always. So when she died, she tried to take me with her."

I brush the hair off of his damp face. "That's not the way life works."

"You think I don't know that now?" There's a bitterness in his voice that tells me he is still more man than spirit. "I didn't ask for this. It was all her doing. We couldn't let each other go."

Remembering the intensity of my emptiness after Scarlet died, and the way it still sneaks up on me, I wonder if I would've done the same if I could. Being so near to Tristan's pain is making my own well up again. I try to push it back but my throat is tightening.

"She never let me go," he says softly.

I lie down beside him. I can't look at his face anymore and I don't want him to see mine if I start to cry. I want a story. A distraction.

"Tell me about her in life."

Though he has stopped crying, his breathing is still hitching in his lungs. The backs of our hands are touching.

"I was a student," he begins. "An... apprentice to an apothecary." He pauses to take a deep breath, trying to steady his voice. "It's odd to remember all this again... I guess I never truly forgot it, it just... became unimportant."

"I suppose it would." I focus on his voice rather than Scarlet's laugh.

"Sort of like... what you had for dinner the night before. It didn't matter anymore the next day. And with no one to converse with, I lost track of who I was completely."

I'm watching the flickering shapes on the ceiling caused by the candles. "I'm glad you remember," I say so quietly that I'm surprised he understands me. "What was her name?"

Tristan takes a deep breath and lets it out shakily. The back of my hand pressed against his is cooling. "Victoria. She lived down the street from the apothecary. I would often see her out and about, selling roses. Her father had a beautiful garden. Their roses were their livelihood."

I can't imagine living in a community where I could make a living selling flowers. Then again, I'm sure some would pay a fortune for a rose now. A single joy before the end.

"She would stop me when I was out on my errands. She would ask me if I wanted to buy a rose. I never had time. The apothecary was very strict and it would've displeased my parents for me to have spoken to someone of such... well, we were meant to be above those who sold their wares on the streets. I paid her no attention for quite a long time, I'm afraid."

The light and shadow on the ceiling is mesmerizing. I imagine the shadows forming the shapes of a lady and a man, acting out the story for me like Scarlet used to do. *Scarlet. No, focus on Tristan*, I tell myself.

"She even came to the shop once, to sell her roses. That's when I realized she wasn't interested in selling at all. She was interested in me." He smiles wistfully. "I'd been so focused on my studies that I hadn't even noticed. The apothecary was watching so I dismissed her. But on the way home, I stopped and paid her handsomely for a red rose."

I see the shadow girl curtsy and hand the man a black flower above me.

"I bought a rose every day so that I could speak with her. We couldn't be seen together for long, so I snuck out to meet her in the moonlight. She was an artist. A painter. Her thoughts were so fascinating to me. I was intently focused on the future. Memorizing herbs and medicines. Parts of the body. Everything had a compartment and place. But she showed me the joy of going for a walk just to be outside, not to get somewhere. Finding new shapes in the stars. Feeling the warmth of the one you love."

I have forgotten that he is part spirit. He is only a young man. I've never heard such talk, least of all from a boy. Then again, the boys of my village are preoccupied with trying to survive. There isn't room for such observations, such story-making. Or is there?

The backs of our hands are still touching. His cool fingers slide over mine then rest against my palm. His hand is warmer.

"My parents didn't approve. She was poor. When I disobeyed them and snuck out to see her, they punished me. I was locked in my room like a prisoner. I was to focus on my studies and forget about her. I tried to, but she never let go of me. She left a rose on the doorstep every day. My mother would stomp on them and bring me the trampled petals. I scattered them all in my bed."

I imagine what that must feel like. To care about someone so much that you surround yourself with whatever you can from them. Sleep and dream with them. I tense as I hear whispers in the corners of my mind. Are they hers? No, they're Tristan's. They're tugging at me. He rests his temple against mine, squeezing my hand.

His whispers envelop me. I close my eyes. When I open them, I am Tristan again. Only this time, I have a proper human mind. I am aware of a dozen things at once, unlike when I was a spirit.

I hear rain falling outside. The constant drizzle has lent me some comfort in my solitary confinement. So long as it's there, I know I am not missing pleasant days in garden paths with Victoria. I am alone in my room with all the lamps burning. The air smells of dust, rain and dried roses. My backside is sore from sitting in this wooden chair for so long. I am at my desk, studying drawings of herbs. Perhaps I should move to the bed. Though what difference will it make?

My chest is heavy. Perpetual nausea tints my belly. I close my eyes. It is late and I am tired, but I have nothing else to do to occupy my time. She's gone and I'll never see her again.

I kick a leg of the desk. That felt good. I have to stop myself to keep from kicking it again. The nausea in my stomach hasn't gone away since my mother first turned the key and locked me in my room. That was a week ago. I'm starting to think that breaking my leg in the inevitable fall out of my second story window will be worth it to escape. I need to move.

The front door downstairs bangs. I tense as I listen. Someone is pounding on the door. It's far too late for callers. No one answers so the pounding continues. I rise and press my ear against my door. Perhaps it's a patient. Someone hoping I can heal them. Who else would be here in wee hours of the morning?

More pounding, then hurried footsteps as my parents get out of bed. The door is opened.

"What are you –" my mother gets out before she screams.

Someone is pushed over and a piece of furniture falls. We're being robbed. We're being robbed and I'm locked up here and can't do anything about it. My father shouts at the bandit to stop. Feet pound up the stairs. They're heading for my door. I back up as the pounding shakes the wood in front of me. What madman would –

"Tristan!"

I know that voice. "Victoria? What are you doing?"

The door shakes. She is ramming it with her shoulder. I can hear my parents arguing as they chase her up the stairs. "Where's the key?" she shouts.

"Leave immediately," my father bellows. My mother shrieks at something.

Victoria rams the door with her shoulder again. My heart is racing. What's going on? Everyone in the hall is shouting at once and I can't tell what any of them are saying. She rams the door again and it busts at the hinges. I just have time to leap away before it crashes to the floor.

Victoria stands before me, panting. Her dark brown hair had been in a bun but is now yanked out in places. Added to her flushed cheeks, she looks wild and beautiful. My mother is behind her in a dressing gown, holding a chamberstick, while my father is trying to shove past her. Victoria smiles as she catches her breath and holds out her hand for mine. That's when I notice that the other holds a large knife.

"Victoria..."

She shakes her hand. "Hurry."

My mother latches onto her arm. "I will not have you barge into our home and –"

Victoria yanks her arm out of my mother's grasp and shoves her away. *Enough.*

I hastily step out into the hall as my father grabs Victoria's hair and yanks. She spins about and slashes with the knife, slicing his arm. He screams.

"Victoria!" I shout. These are my parents. She can't just –

She latches onto my arm and shoves me in front of her, towards the stairs. I see my mother notice my father's blood out of the corner of my eye.

"Murderer!" she shouts.

I try to stop at the top of the stairs. I want to see if my father is all right, but Victoria shoves me. "Move, Tristan!"

"Mother, don't –" I get out before she screams and flings hot candle wax into Victoria's face. Victoria shouts and lets go of me with a shove. Grabbing onto the wall, I stop myself from falling down the stairs then look over my shoulder to see what's going on.

Victoria and my mother are grabbing each other's arms. My father is huddled in the corner, cradling his arm, his sleeve stained red. I must aid him. I take a step towards him when the candle snuffs out. My mother screams and a body goes tumbling past me. It knocks my feet out from under me and I fall, landing so hard on the stairs that I can't breathe for a moment.

My father is shouting. Someone is moaning. Hands are yanking at me but I can't move. I can't move until I finally force air into my lungs. My chest is burning as my shoulders are yanked off the stair. Strong arms help me to my feet and we hurry down the staircase.

"No..." someone moans at the bottom of the landing and I realize it's my mother.

Victoria has ahold of me like a force of nature. She yanks open the front door. The drizzle is now a downpour outside.

"You harlot, he's my son!" my mother yells as we run out the door. "My son!"

The rain is cold and the street is slippery but I keep pace with Victoria. I keep pace with her because I don't know what else to do. What did she just do? What did *we* just do?

I'm soaked by the time I stop running. She yanks on my hands to keep me going but I don't budge. We're outside of a stranger's house and the lamp in the window makes Victoria's face partially visible. Her hair is plastered all over it but still I can see that her cheek is pink from the candlewax. I shake my head. "Victoria –"

Before I know it, her cold hands are on either side of my face and her lips are against mine. She is kissing me with such hunger that I begin to feel warm. I kiss her back, my hands digging into her wet hair. I only stop when she starts laughing, which makes me laugh. Her touch is making me forget that what she did was wrong.

I shake my head again. "My father..."

"We're free now, Tristan." She kisses me once more. "We're free."

Free. Yes, we are free. I have longed to be free. I just never realized how intimidating freedom was. Victoria, on the other hand, seems intoxicated by it. "We have nowhere to go," I whisper.

She pulls a pouch of gold coins out of her dress. She has robbed my parents. "We can go anywhere."

I smile. I know I shouldn't, I know what we're doing is reproachable, but I can't help it. We truly are our own masters now. Snatching the knife back up, she takes my hand in hers again and we run into the night, like blackbirds taking flight.

Suddenly we are at a tree. A naked ash kissed by the moonlight. The air is frigid and the hoary ground fog around us glows eerily. I am filled with both delight and anxiety. Victoria is grinning at me, her breath clouding before her in crystalline puffs. She has twined roses into her hair.

"I pledge myself to you," she says, taking my hand in hers. "From this life to the next."

She has such affection in her eyes. I am the most blessed man in the world for I am all she sees. I never would've imagined someone could love me so much to fight for me like she has. It makes me feel small and light, as if I am that spot of moonlight in her eyes. I rest my hand on hers. "From this life to the next," I say.

Together, we slip on a bracelet woven of dried reeds and round, red berries. We are bound together. We are wed.

I kiss my wife. She slips her hand under my vest and snakes it up my back. Her touch is so warm, her lips so bedewed with passion that I want more. The blood rushing past my ears sounds like the rush of a wave as we lie down.

Now we're in an abandoned house. Most of the roof has fallen in and lies mildewing on the floor. I look over the meager supplies that we've procured here and there. If we spend too much gold at once, vendors will mark our faces. We don't dare travel on the main roads, either. The risk of being robbed by highwaymen and losing all we have is far too great.

Victoria is lying on our quilt upon the floor, her long brown hair pulled back in a braid. Her black dress is stained with dust and drops of water, her purple shawl is moth-eaten. It pains me to see her so tattered and filthy. She is my wife and I am meant to care for her, but she refuses to bathe.

She has lain like this all day, chewing on her grimy nails. At first I thought she was tired from traveling. Goodness knows, we're both hungry and cold these days. However nothing I offer can make her rise. She warned me once that she has spells. I am certain this is one of them.

We have already been here for hours and need to keep going if we're to make the next village by nightfall, but she is content not to budge.

"Victoria?" She doesn't respond and I sigh. Lying down behind her, I rest my arm on her waist. "Won't you tell me what ails you?"

She shakes her head no. While I am slightly irritated by her childishness, I keep my impatience at bay for it won't help the situation any. I am realizing now that my wife is not balanced. I rub her arm, reminding her that I am present.

"You can tell me anything," I whisper. I kiss the back of her neck.

She turns to look at me, and the frightened expression on her face makes her small mouth look tight, her brown eyes hollow, as if she is someone else. "It's you," she squeaks.

"What?"

She rests a dirty hand on my cheek and strokes it. I smile at her touch for she hasn't touched me in days. Tears are pooling in her eyes.

"It's you," she whispers again. I rest my hand on hers, holding it to my cheek. "I want you so much that I feel I could die."

I chuckle. "I'm right here, darling."

"But you won't always be. You'll die. I'll die."

Such dark thoughts are unfit for a young bride. What could have brought on such worries?

"I want you," she repeats. She is holding my face tighter, pinching my cheek so that it hurts. I have never seen her like this before. "Always."

"Then I shall be with you always," I whisper. My words don't seem to have comforted her. If anything, her grip on me is tighter. I wince and try to tug her hand away. "Victoria..."

"I wish we were the same person," she says in a rush. She won't let go and is now holding onto my hair. "You could live inside of me, forever. Safe. Where no one could ever take you from me again. Not your parents. Not even death." Tears slip out of her eyes.

"You're hurting me." I let go of her hand and rest mine on her arm. Her muscles are so flexed that her skin is solid, causing my heart to leap in alarm.

"I love you more than my life," she continues. Her dry lips press against mine as she kisses me. She won't let go of my hair and my scalp is burning. "I don't want to eat." She kisses me again. "Sleep." Another kiss. "Drink. I just want you," she murmurs against my lips, scooting closer to me. Her fingernails dig into my scalp with sharp stings.

"Victoria!"

She startles at my shout and releases me, her eyes growing wide as if she didn't realize what she had been doing. I screw my eyes shut as she pulls her hand away. When I open them again, I see her studying my torn hair sticking to her fingers with anguish. "I'm sorry," she whispers. Her frightened eyes meet mine. "I'm so sorry," she sobs.

My scalp is still prickling and though I want to be mad at her, she looks so pitiful. My anger dissolves as her tears slip down her cheeks.

"I'm so sorry," she repeats over and over. I pull her into my chest and rub her back as she cries. "I'm so sorry..."

I am unsettled. She isn't my wife right now. She is someone else. But as she wraps her arms and legs around me, as she kisses my neck while she weeps, I don't mind. She may be unbalanced, but the unbalance is in my favor.

Now we are in a town. Lamps glow in windows. It is night and hand in hand, we weave through the streets. I am carrying our pack and my arm is beginning to ache from the weight. Victoria's shawl is over her hair but I know it does little to warm her.

We enter a tavern and pay with gold. The keeper empties his lockbox to give us our change in silver. I know we've drawn attention but it's too cold to sleep outside tonight and the wealthy often visit such establishments. Victoria is in good spirits and I want her to remain in such a state for as long as possible.

Upstairs, we bathe then lie in bed. She falls asleep with her head on my bare chest, her ear resting above my heart where she can hear it beating. It is her favorite way to sleep. My spine sags against the mattress as my weight is lifted off of my body. How I have missed the comforts of a home.

I wake before Victoria. Though half of my chest is cold without my shirt, the half with her on it is warm. I sigh. We need a home of our own. We're currently four towns away from the city. If we could put a few more between us then no one would ever find us.

Heavy feet pound on the stair. "Second on the right," the keep shouts.

Never mind. Someone already has found us. *Blast.* I shove Victoria off of me, roughly waking her up as I climb out of bed. We only have the knife so I yank it out of our pack. Victoria gets out of bed, wrapping the blanket around her thin nightclothes.

"Tristan?"

I step in front of her as the footsteps pause outside the door. She screams as the door is kicked in. I keep her behind me with one hand and hold the knife out in the other. The man who kicked the door in is wearing a fine vest and jacket and is clean-shaven. He is from the city. He smirks as he surveys us so obviously caught unawares. "Now how would you two ragamuffins come across a piece of gold?"

The keep must've alerted him when he heard he was hunting for two thieves. We were right to stay off the roads. I shift my grip on the knife, readying to throw it if provoked. "We have no quarrel with you. Leave us."

The man cocks his head. "What're you going to do?" He laughs. If the door falling hadn't woken up the other tenants, his booming voice will have. "Stick me with your little knife? You don't have it in you, boy."

I want to throw the knife and stab him in the heart just to spite him. He pulls his jacket aside and lifts out a crossbow. Casually adjusting the bolt on the string, he aims it at me.

"Tristan," Victoria whispers as she presses herself against my back.

I try to swallow but my throat is dry. That bolt could pierce through me and into Victoria, killing us both. After several tense moments, I set aside the knife.

"All right," I say. Lifting my hands to show the man I mean him no harm, I crouch by our sack and tug out the bag of coins. I toss them onto the bed as I rise. "Take it. You can see for yourself that we've hardly spent any."

The man glances at the coins and arches his brow, then grabs the sack and tucks it into his jacket. His crossbow is still aimed on me.

"I thank you kindly," he says, his voice gravely. "But I don't think you quite understand the predicament you find yourself in. I'm not here just to take back your parents' gold. You've soiled your family's name. You're no longer their heir, their son. They want you gone." He shifts his grip on his crossbow. "And I'm here to see their wishes fulfilled. On you and your little tramp." He looks what he can see of Victoria up and down with a callous eye. "Though I don't see why I can't have some fun with her first."

How dare he.

I take a step towards him and feel Victoria's hand try to snatch mine and fail. "She is my wife," I snarl.

He laughs. "You're just a boy. A woman like that needs a man."

Victoria scoffs behind me. I try to ignore his taunts but they're flooding my veins with animosity.

The man scowls. "All right then. Have fun watching your boy die."

He fires the crossbow.

I don't know how, but I've lunged to the side just in time. The bolt shatters the glass of the window. Victoria screams. I'm not thinking properly. The man is much larger than me, but I charge at him all the same. He reaches into his jacket for another bolt but I tackle him onto the floor before he can get it out.

"Tristan!" Victoria shouts.

The man shoves me off and pins me beneath him. He reaches in his jacket again and I realize he has grabbed a knife, then his hand is like iron around my throat. I kick at his groin and he screams. He backhands me so hard that everything goes black and I feel as if I'm falling. Then little pinpricks of golden light shoot across my vision as the darkness fades. I regain my senses just in time to see him readying the knife above my heart.

I grab his wrist and shove but he is stronger than me. Gritting my teeth, I press with all my might but the tip of the blade is digging into my chest. He starts to laugh as he presses down harder. Then his laugh turns into a gurgle.

My face and torso are sprayed with a shower of warm liquid. His knife slips and slices across my abdomen. Warmth rushes out of me. Blood. My blood. His blood. He grabs at something sticking out of his throat and I realize it's the tip of a knife. After gasping for a few breaths, he collapses on top of me.

Victoria is standing behind him, her eyes wide. His blood is dripping down my face and I have to blink as I catch my breath, staring up at her. My abdomen is just now beginning to burn.

"We have to leave," Victoria whispers.

She dashes out of view and I can hear her gathering our belongings. I struggle out from under the dead man and shout when the muscles of my stomach flare in fire upon using them. It takes me a moment to catch my breath once I'm out from under the corpse, but Victoria is already at my side. She kicks the dead man over and scowls as she retrieves our sack of gold.

I climb to my feet, clutching my abdomen. Blood is slicking my hand, trickling down past my belly button, staining my trousers. I'm alarmed by how fast it's leaking from me. Victoria shoulders our pack then moves to rush out only to stop once she sees my wound. She lets out a surprised gasp.

Tenants are sticking their heads out of their doors. We cannot linger. I hold out my other hand and Victoria takes it. Together, we once again flee.

The woods are before us.

"That's when we came here."

The voice is mine. Tristan's. No, I'm not Tristan, I remind myself as the images fade and the whispers quiet. I am Willow. Tristan is speaking to me now. His voice is soft.

"We ran for days. Well... we tried. My wound slowed us. I became fevered. I was able to tell her what plants could help me. She took care of me. When I was stronger, we found this glen and decided to stay. So I built this house for us."

I am listening, but I am also moving each of my limbs one at a time. Reminding myself that I am me. That I've never really seen such a city. Such rooms, such people.

The candle shadows are still flickering above us. Tristan's hand is warm in mine. I turn my head to look at him, but his gaze is on the ceiling. As I study his profile, I realize I will never be able to think of him the same way again. I know too much. And now that he remembers, he knows too much. Or at least, he knows. I take a deep breath and let it out shakily.

I let the memories he just shared with me trickle through my mind as I try to make sense of them. I find myself distracted by the line of his nose, the curves of his lips, the darkness of his lashes. And I realize with a start that I am like her. I want him. I have always wanted him.

Chapter Fourteen

I force myself to look away from his profile. My heart is beating as if I'd just run. I'm not like her. I can't be. But I am. He really is the most handsome man I have ever seen. I was too focused on the task at hand before to have paid much attention to my own thoughts, but like Victoria, one look into those mischievously vulnerable eyes and I was lost.

Closing my eyes, I am filled with disgust. I could never become so drunk on him as Victoria had, could I? So wound up in my passion and lust that I forced him to remain with me against his will? That I hurt him just to be with him?

I'm yanked out of my mind as he pulls my hand up to his chest and envelops it in both of his, hugging it. I can feel his heart slowly beating. His heart that still belongs to her. The woman who is doing exactly what she said she would – trapping him inside of her to keep forever.

My guts wrench and for a moment I worry I'll be sick. Of all my thoughts and theories about the corpse, I never once thought that we could be similar.

Tristan's chest rises and falls beneath my hand locked in his. I'm afraid to look at him. Afraid he'll cast some spell on me. Afraid I'll cast some spell on myself. Afraid my wanting of him will be my failure. He is still her pawn. He is still a victim that I need to protect. A spirit that needs my help as a Listener. A man who needs my help as another human being. And she is an abomination.

I think of how ill she made herself with her love for him. So lovesick that she couldn't even rouse herself to enjoy him, even when he was at her side. Tristan had considered her unbalanced, but he too was blinded by his affection for her. Victoria was more than unbalanced, as is evidenced by what her spirit has become. She was unhinged.

I've been around damaged people before. Their behavior is so drastic and confusing that their families become exhausted caring for them. Though he may not have understood it when she was alive, that's what Victoria was. Even then she was sucking away his life and energy. Maybe she couldn't help it in life, but she can now. And she hasn't changed.

Such people disgust me. I should have more sympathy for the unbalanced, but I don't. Maybe because I worry I am one myself. I didn't used to be. But ever since I lost my sister, I've been behaving as if I don't have anything to lose. I've been such a fool. Of course I still have something to lose. I have everything to lose, least of all being my life.

I really am unbalanced. Why else would I volunteer to be sacrificed?

I told myself I did it because I'd heard whispers in the woods and thought I could fix things. That was part of it, sure. But there was a part of me I never wanted to acknowledge. A part of me that wanted to leave the world of the living and join Scarlet. That part made me ignore my family instead of saying goodbye to them one last time after the ceremony. It made me think of Draven as a coward for not saying something that he never needed to say in the first place.

But being here with Tristan has made me forget about that part of me. Maybe because I'm holding hands with someone whose half-dead so I feel like I'm half in the Netherworld already. And maybe I am. I've accomplished what I had hoped for. I am lost to my family.

To Draven, my dearest friend. And what's worse, his last memories of me are of hurt.

Tears blur my vision. I am weak. I am cruel. Why did I think I was better than the corpse? I'm the same. An animated body, dead to all around her except a half-spirit who's deader than me.

Tristan hasn't said anything for some time. I look over at him and his eyes are shut, his breathing even. I didn't know he even needed sleep. Maybe he didn't before, but now that he's more human, he needs rest. I need rest, as well.

Experiencing his memories and fighting off my own has drained me. The fire is dying down. My hand is still resting in his, on his chest. I curl up on my side and tuck my chin into his shoulder, hugging him with my free arm. I let his body heat warm me, and soon I fall asleep.

I am startled awake hours later by Tristan jerking up. "What?" he hisses.

The lamps are still lit. I wince and rub the sleep out of my eyes as I sit up. He looks around, confused, then his eyes settle on me.

"What just happened? Why am I on the floor?"

"You fell asleep," I say, stretching my sore body. Wood isn't all that comfortable.

"Asleep...." He runs his hands through his hair, drawing his knees up to his chest. "I haven't slept in so long." He grins. "I had a dream. I can't remember the last time I dreamt."

"What was it?"

He has that childish look of wonder in his eyes again. A look that I know will draw me in. So instead, I pick at dirt under my fingernails.

"I felt the sun on my face," he whispers. "We were in a meadow. Wildflowers were blooming all around. And the butterflies, oh, the butterflies were every different color of the rainbow."

I hope he doesn't notice that I'm avoiding looking at him.

"But instead of being jealous of them, I thought that they must be envious of me. My time on this earth with a body may be briefer than theirs, but it was long enough to feel the sun. To feel your hand."

I look at him then. His eyes are smiling. Warm.

"Can you imagine how glorious the sun will feel when it returns?"

I smile a little but can't hold his gaze long. I am still sickened by my realization last night and don't want him to see. Don't want him to know that I am like her.

"Is something troubling you?"

I take a deep breath and let it out. "Tristan, I..." I mean to tell him that I am scared. That I feel safe around him. That I think he's beautiful. But instead, something bitter comes out. "How could you still love her?"

He blinks. "She's my wife."

"She was."

"From this life, to the next. I showed you."

"I know." My hair is falling out of its pins so I let it down and it tickles my shoulders. "But look at all she does to you."

A line forms between his brows. "She has to hurt me. It's how she gains her strength. And if she doesn't have strength, she can't stay here with me."

"But she's not here with you. She's in the house, sure. But do you ever spend time together when she isn't hurting you? Do you ever speak?"

He shakes his head. "She can't speak anymore."

"She spoke to me."

Tristan looks away, his hair falling into his face. "You're a Listener."

"Not like that. She used her voice. Or what's left of her voice. When she tied me up."

Tristan stares at the wall, his jaw is taut. I look away.

"Do you ever wonder," I begin quietly, "why she doesn't use fire as you do to heal?"

"It isn't powerful enough."

"How do you know?"

"It just isn't," he snaps, climbing to his feet and crossing over to the ashes in the fireplace. He crouches and begins to prod them back to life.

“I saw what she did to you when she was sick. Do you ever think she might hurt you on purpose?”

Tristan stops poking at the fire. “Of course not.”

“Sometimes we’re blinded by –”

“Everything she has ever done was because she loved me,” he snips over his shoulder.

I’m silenced for a moment. He’s never used such a tone. “I don’t doubt that,” I say quietly. “But I think she hurt you because she loved you. So much that she didn’t know what to do with such a powerful feeling. Because she was more than unbalanced, Tristan. You must know that now.”

He lets his knees touch the floor then eases onto his haunches, his expression one of intense concern as he stares at the boards below him. “I know,” he whispers.

“It’s all right to be angry with her. That doesn’t mean you love her any less. But you can’t keep thinking that what’s happening is all right. It isn’t. You don’t deserve that.”

“I *showed* you,” he says, looking me in the eye. “She loved me so much that she killed for me. She would’ve done anything for me.”

“Except let you live.”

Tristan sucks in a breath, as if to argue, but instead looks back at the floor. “You don’t understand. No one had ever wanted me like that before. Not even my parents. And she’s all I have.”

“Tristan?” It takes a few moments but he eventually turns to look at me. “You have me.”

The forlornness in his eyes begins to ebb as he gazes at me. He blinks and starts to smile. Then all the lights in the house go out.

And I realize what a huge mistake I’ve made by admitting I care about him. She has glimpsed how I feel. I’ve practically handed her the deadliest weapon she could wield.

Tristan is no longer her pawn to play games with me. He is her means to torture me into surrender.

Chapter Fifteen

I leap to my feet, tearing the hem of Victoria's gown. I hurry over to the fireplace, the only source of light, but Tristan is gone. I glance about, hunting for where he could've hidden. She couldn't have fed on him so much that he lost his body already.

"Tristan?"

His breathing tickles my shoulder and I turn around. Only to yelp. There before me is the corpse. Victoria.

I stumble backwards. Her funerary shrouds are drifting about her, empty sockets boring into mine. Her yellowed teeth look like they're grinning.

I square my shoulders. "Where is he?"

She clacks her jaw, startling me. Gagging noises, like a vomiting cat come out of her throat. Amidst them, I can make out one word. "Mine."

"I know who you are."

Victoria's bone-hand darts out from behind the shrouds and yanks a strap of the gown off so quickly that I yelp again. My shoulder burns and I grab the strap and yank away to keep her from taking the dress off. I'm bleeding where her long nails have scraped against my skin. Someone cries out in a corner of the house. *Tristan.*

I sneer at her. "You're a coward. A selfish coward."

She clacks her jaws again. Tristan screams and I cover my ears because he sounds like he's drowning in his own blood.

"Leave him alone," I snarl.

A rattling sound comes from her chest. She wheezes out a breath and this time she does stink like rotting animal. "Mine," she manages again.

"What you're doing is killing my people," I shout. "My family."

The corpse cocks her head. "I don't care," she wheezes.

Tristan's noises no longer sound human. I grab a burning branch from the fire and wield it in front of me. She hisses and darts back quicker than I thought possible, slipping into the shadows. I thrust the makeshift torch about but can't see her. Of course she would abandon her body at the first sign that I was willing to burn it. The fiend.

Tristan's screaming stops. The lamps come on. I keep the torch in front of me as I spin about, making sure she's gone. Then I spot Tristan at the top of the stairs. The side of his face is oozing blood out of gashes from his old wound once again and he's clinging to the bars of the railing as if on a ship in a squall. Casting the torch back into the fire, I start to run to him then stop myself. The stairs. Her easiest trap.

He is shaking. That much I can tell from here. Holding onto the rails, he stiffly rises. Tristan is about to take a step down when something hits him from behind. He's too weak to stop himself and falls, hitting each step with a sickening thump.

Crack. A bone breaks.

When he lands in a heap at the bottom, he doesn't move. I'm about to run to him when he lets out a noise that makes me shiver. A moan that sounds like groaning wood and the bleat of a hooved animal.

Something's wrong. My body hair is standing on end and I take a step back. He presses his palms on the floor and raises his head to lock eyes with me. Through the blood on his face, I can only see one clearly. For a moment, his gaze is frightened, even as his mouth forms into a sneer.

"Run," he growls. Then his eyes are darkened with malice. He doesn't look like Tristan anymore.

I run as fast as I can on my healing ankle. With a roar, he chases after me. I try the front door but it's still locked. I bolt into the dining room, knocking over chairs as I pass. I don't know what's going on. He is fast. Faster than me.

"You killed her," he screams.

I glance over my shoulder as I enter the kitchen and he leaps over the fallen chairs with ease. I overturn the rough table and grab the same knife that I picked up the first time I entered this room.

Tristan skids to a halt as he reaches the table. He tries to circle, to lunge at me, but I leap to the other side. He is panting and has a manic glint in his eyes. The expression is so foreign on his face that I hurl a pot at him.

He bats it out of the way and lunges at me again. I shriek as he catches my arm, but he's still on the other side of the table. I wrestle away from him and dart out of the room. I nearly trip over the fallen chairs, and am about to head up the stairs when I remember that I can't.

Whirling about to face him, I realize he hasn't followed me into the parlor. I back away from the foot of the stairs, slowly. My naked heel slips on something. A small pool of blood. His blood.

Leaping away, I listen. My pulse is racing and I can't catch my breath.

Something falls in the kitchen. He must still be in there. Slowly side-stepping, I inch over to the entryway. I can see the corner of the kitchen. There is a shadow there. He seems to be standing still. Listening to me.

I close my mouth and breathe through my nose so that I can better listen then inch a little closer to the middle so that I can see more.

No. No he's not in the kitchen anymore. Where did he –

He flies at me out of nowhere. His body slams into mine and I'm tackled onto my back. My head hits the floor with a thud and I see pinpricks of light as he climbs on top of me. His hands grope my neck. He means to strangle me. I grab his wrists and try to pry them off.

"You killed her," he screams again. His brown eyes are tinted red.

"No!" I shove. His icy thumbs are digging into my flesh, bruising my windpipe. I start kicking. Blood drips from his face onto mine.

"You killed her."

He is trapped in his own anger.

"She died," I choke out. "Years ago. Remember?"

The darting lights are coming back. The knife is still in my hand, so I ram the butt into the side of his head as hard as I can. His grip relaxes as he slumps off of me, landing on his side. I gasp, trying to force air into my swollen throat, sitting up and making the lights dance more furiously. I rest a hand to my neck as I force in another squeaky breath then scoot away from his body. He is unconscious but I still don't want to be within reach.

The lamps go out. I swear I can hear a woman laughing upstairs behind the chained door.

I sit still for some time, until I don't feel lightheaded anymore. Then I grab the low table to help me to my feet. I am filled with a cold sickness. He tried to kill me. Tears are blurring my vision as I back away from his still form, his back to me.

A part of me knows that I should've expected this. That he is still part spirit and that spirits get caught up in their passions. This is why spirits shouldn't have bodies. But he had seemed so living. And he was my friend. Now I'm alone. I allow myself to cry. My neck is bruising. Why did I trust him? Why does he have to be half dead?

I scoot into the far corner of the room against the outside wall and hug myself. It's some time before my tears stop. I'm not only crying for how frightened he made me. I'm crying because I'm trapped here. Because my little brother is starving. Because Scarlet died. Because Lady died. Because I haven't seen the sun in five years. Because I'm tired of being brave and alone.

The fire suddenly dims. Tristan stirs.

Pulling my knees up closer to my chest, my cheeks still wet with tears, I feel like a little girl again but don't care. I want my big sister. Not this man. Not this deceptive, turbulent man. He can keep his corpse bride.

I see Tristan's silhouette as he sits up and gingerly touches the side of his head. He wipes away what he can of the blood. By the callous way he is touching his injuries, I know he has healed himself. He huddles by the fire for a moment, hugging his knees. Tristan rocks back and forth for a while then suddenly stiffens. I'm worried he's angry again and I tense. Then he looks about, as if he has lost something. I shrink a little when he spots me in the corner. Dried blood is smeared, darkening half of his face.

"Don't come near me," I say lowly.

His eyes are wide and deer-like but no amount of beauty could draw me back to them right now. Not after I saw them gleam with such malice. He starts to scoot towards me.

"Don't," I bark and he stops.

"Oh, Willow," he whispers. "Are you very hurt?"

It still pains me to breathe but I doubt there will be any permanent damage. Not to my body, at least. His expression is full of remorse. I don't want to stop being angry with him. I rest my cheek on my arm, looking away.

"I'm so very sorry," he whispers. "I don't know what got into me." His voice cracks but I'm still not going to look. "I couldn't stop myself. I was so filled with rage... you must hate me."

I don't answer. Let him think what he will. So long as he keeps his distance. I know he's watching me. Waiting for me to alleviate his guilt by doing what he always does when Victoria hurts him. Forgive and forget. Not me. Not now. I'll never get so wrapped up in another that I lose my own will.

"I could fetch you some water," he offers quietly. "Some food?"

I'm quite comfortable how I am. I don't budge. Let him feel his regret. Let him learn his lesson.

After some time, he rises. I shift to rest my forehead against my crossed arms, hiding my face. He's lighting some of the candles and lamps and I like the darkness of my own little cave. By the sounds of it, he's going about the house and straightening up. I hear him right the chairs and table. Tidy up the kitchen. Clean the blood off the floor.

It takes him some time and I am content in my hiding spot. Comfortable. Even though my shoulder is burning where Victoria scratched me open. As the shock fades, I think back on what happened. At least I'd had some warning beforehand. I could sense his anger building. It won't catch me off guard again. And he had warned me, as well, I realize. Before his eyes took on that horrible glint, they had been his. He had told me to run. If he knew what was coming, if he could feel the hatred building inside, then it wasn't his. Spirits trapped in their passion don't realize they're trapped. Which means it was her.

I close my eyes and let out a breath. Of course it was her. What better way to make me give up than to have my last shred of hope pulled out from under me? I know Tristan. I know him boiled down to his purest form, his simplest essence. He would never hurt me on his own. Even when he was more spirit than man, he wasn't one to become trapped inside himself. I feel more stable now that I am certain his attack was her doing. I just wish it wasn't his hands that did it.

Tristan comes back into the room. I know he's standing just a few feet from me and wonder if he knows what I know. He sets something down beside me then stokes the fire.

"Enough is enough," he says quietly. "Thank you for all you've done for me, but I'm afraid it's not working. I'll never be human again."

He walks away so quietly that I don't realize he's moving until one of the floorboards squeaks in the dining room.

I pull my head up then. He blames himself. Not her. Which isn't right. I should tell him that he tried to warn me. He has set a goblet of water near me. Reaching out for it, I take a sip. It isn't just water. There's some sort of dried plant in it, as well. He remembers his apothecary recipes. It soothes my throat. I'm ready to talk now.

I take a deep breath and let it out. It doesn't hurt, but my joints ache as I slowly force myself up. I'm about to follow him into the kitchen when I hear a bang. It startles me. That selfish excuse for a woman won't give us a moment's peace. The sound came from the kitchen which isn't lit well. I hobble forward and see twin grotesque shadows from separate candles swaying on the wall. The bang wasn't Victoria at all. Tristan has hanged himself.

Chapter Sixteen

I run to the kitchen and kick aside a stool that I realize he used to get high enough. Tristan's eyes are closed and he isn't breathing. He isn't fighting. I grab his legs and try lifting him. I know he can reform his body after having lost it, but his body has never died before. I don't know what will happen if it does.

"Tristan!"

His legs keep slipping. I'm not strong enough. I let go and right the stool before sprinting back into the parlor and retrieving my knife. By the time I reach the kitchen again, his skin is ashen white, his lips blue. Climbing on the stool, I hiss as my ankle complains. Then I hack at the rope. It snaps and he hits the ground hard, making me wince. I didn't think of that part.

Hopping back down, I cut the rope off his neck. The skin there is already yellowing with bruising. I feel his pulse. It takes me a while to find it but when I do, I gasp in relief. It's faint and floundering but there.

Now that he's hit his head twice in a few hours, I feel guilty for striking him before, but I had to. I throw the rope in the hearth. I need to get him near the fire so he can heal himself when he comes to.

I break a sweat doing so, but I manage to drag him back into the parlor, in front of the flames. I refill the goblet. Wetting my hand, I pat his face and try to wake him. It doesn't work. His skin isn't as pale but his lips are still purple. His hands are like ice but that's not something new.

"Tristan?"

There's nothing else I can do, so I grab a cloth and gently clean the dried blood off of his face and hands. As I do, it gets harder and harder to breathe. Not because of my throat. Because of my chest. Because of what he said before he tried to kill himself. Because of what I didn't say.

I left him alone with his guilt. His terrible guilt thinking that he'd attacked me of his own will. I hadn't intended to be cruel. I wasn't thinking clearly. But I'd done it all the same. I start crying again. I hate crying. It gives me a headache and exhausts me, yet still, I rest my forehead on Tristan's chest and weep.

Maybe he was right. Maybe he will never be human again. He is still spirit enough for her to attack him like she did, to turn him against me. Then again, we all exist as both body and spirit. In life, the body is more important. It's our spirit house. I was trying to help Tristan to that point of balance. He thinks we failed. But Victoria seems to think we're succeeding. Why else would she try so desperately to stop me?

Mine, she had said. She was claiming Tristan as hers. I'm taking him away from her. As I saw in his memory of her near-kidnapping of him, she was willing to do whatever it took to keep him. She killed that bounty hunter to protect him. No, not him...

I am looking at his face again, half-turned towards me, his features haloed in golden firelight. It wasn't him she was protecting, was it? It was herself and her possessions.

Victoria wanted Tristan for her own. She couldn't even share him with his parents. She wanted him for the sake of having him, not loving him. She may have thought that was love, but looking at him now, I realize it wasn't. He was like a rose to her. A thing of beauty for her to prune and pick and set upon a shelf to gaze at.

Her suffocating addiction to him not only overwhelmed her to the point of hurting him, but Tristan as well. His parents were unaffectionate and strict, yes. But they were right to have tried to protect him from Victoria. Their disapproval of her and Tristan's relationship may have had nothing to do with her being poor and everything to do with her being out of control.

But Tristan was so blinded by his feelings for her, and is still, that he doesn't see the truth. Victoria has always been dangerous. It's only now, after years of torture, that he can admit it, but only to a point. He doesn't like that she hurts him but he won't blame her for it. He won't acknowledge her selfishness, her cruelty. He is loyal to a woman who never existed.

I saw into his mind. I felt how he felt at the time. Empty and restrained until she came along. He mistook her manic desire for passion for him. And I suppose it was passion for him, but in the wrong way. He was too young and too wooed by her fire to notice. Never in any of those memories did she ask him what he wanted. Never did she express an interest in hearing his thoughts. In finding out how he saw the world. Her fascination in him was surface only.

Through her "spells" of lovesickness, her depression over her own obsession with him, she turned his kindness against him. She manipulated his innocence and inexperience. She used her affection as a weapon, withholding it until loneliness overtook him, then giving it back copiously. He would be so grateful that he would willingly forget that she was the one who had made him feel empty in the first place.

That isn't love. That's lust and mania.

And as much as he forgives her, as much as he claims he loves her, part of Tristan knows this isn't right. That it never was right. But after all they had been through together, what other choice could he have had but to remain with Victoria? The hurt of knowing your own mother and father wanted you dead would be hard enough to bear. On top of it, he was alone in the woods, at least a half a day from our village. And all he had was a mad woman.

Tristan groans, yanking me out of my thoughts. One of his legs twitches then he groans again, scrunching up his face. He's trying to wake up. I grab his hand. "Tristan?"

His hand squeezes mine then his eyes flutter open. He winces. I wait as he adjusts to the pain in his body, then smile when his eyes find mine. His lips grow taut and he tugs his hand away. Sighing, he lolls his head to the side, looking at the hearth, but he doesn't move and he doesn't speak.

"I'm glad you're still here," I whisper. He blinks but doesn't respond. "I don't know what I'd have done here alone." His vest is crumpled so I tug on the hem, gently straightening it.

"You'd have lived in peace," he murmurs huskily. His throat is swollen. He's intentionally not healing himself, forcing himself to feel the pain.

"I'd have lived in loneliness."

"I can't hurt you if I'm gone."

I take his hand again and fight him when he tries to pull it away. "That wasn't you, Tristan. You tried to warn me before it happened. It was her."

He stops trying to pull his hand out of mine and holds still for several moments as he considers this.

"Still," he says, then winces as he turns his head to look at me. "I couldn't stop her from taking over me. I never could." He takes a deep breath and sighs. "You should have let me die. I might hurt you again."

"I know," I whisper. "But that's a risk I'm willing to take."

"What if I'm not?"

"You have to. If we give into her now, she'll win. She'll devour your spirit. And the darkness will only spread."

Tristan slides his fingers along mine, examining them. "Then what I did was very selfish. It wouldn't have fixed anything."

"That's why I stopped you."

He stops playing with my hand and I wish he hadn't. He meets my gaze with sad eyes. "I wish I could heal you."

"Why don't you heal yourself instead?"

Tristan shakes his head no and winces. His lips sneer and for a moment I'm worried he'll be sick. After several shallow breaths, the nausea seems to pass. I wonder if he's keeping his necklace of bruises because I still have mine. That is the sort of thing Victoria would say was fair.

"Please? If she attacks you again, you need to be strong."

He sighs then after a while, the fire dims. The dark marks on his neck fade and he sits up.

"Better?"

He nods, his hair falling into his face. I wrap my arm around his and he stiffens, as if unsure of what I'm doing.

"I thought you remembered hugs."

Tristan smiles a little and rests his temple on my shoulder. I lean my cheek against his head. He smells of autumn leaves. "I remember more than hugs," he whispers.

I know. I saw it in his memories. I wonder why he bothered to say it. Is he thinking about more than hugs? Focus. I need to know how much he understands his marriage. "Did you know that our spirits are the most important parts of ourselves?"

"Important?"

"Like you. You've always been very kind."

He shifts to make his cheek more comfortable. "Do you know what your spirit is like?"

My spirit? I've never considered that before.

"It's warm," Tristan says quietly. "And welcoming, like a hearth. Like a mother."

I never would've thought of myself as a mother before. In fact, after the darkness came, I didn't think I'd live long enough to have children at all.

"But more than that," he continues, "it's light. Like the sun. Guiding like the North Star. Strong and unwavering."

My throat has gone dry so I swallow. "You can feel my spirit?"

I feel him shift to peer up at me. "I always have. Since I saw you on the rock." He pulls away and I straighten. "I didn't say hello," he chides himself. "I was so rude."

"You led me to this house. It was probably difficult enough for you to focus on that."

"Forgetful..."

"You were asking for my help. Even if you didn't know it at the time."

"I only wanted a friend."

"That's not all you wanted. I know what you showed me, Tristan. What you and Victoria had – what you *have* – isn't love."

His mouth twitches and he looks away, as if I'm saying something mutinous.

"It's obsession. It's passion, yes, and loyalty on your part, but it isn't love."

He pivots so that his back is to me. "You know that, Tristan," I whisper.

"How could I?" he asks. "When she's all I've ever known?"

"You know yourself. You wouldn't have done this to her if your roles were switched. Would you?"

His shoulders slump. "No."

"Then trust that. Trust yourself. You're not her. You're an individual. She loved parts of you but not all of you. If she did, she'd have waited for you in the Netherworld. She'd have wanted you to live and enjoy your life. Without her."

Even as I'm saying it, I'm realizing that I was wrong to have thought I was like Victoria. I may have never really been in love, but I've felt its pull. I've felt desire. Even trapped here in a house with Tristan, whose appearance gives me such pleasure, I haven't tried to use my ability as a Listener to trick him. I didn't manipulate him when he was simple. I haven't made him do anything against his will. Because he is his own person. He deserves respect. And whatever we may have in common, I admire him for our differences. He's more present than I am. He dwells in the here and now, even after he has remembered his past. Though he is tortured and abused, he isn't jaded. Tristan isn't quietness. He is resilience.

He's looking at me over his shoulder now with such intensity that he must be realizing the same. That what he had was over. That Victoria has kept him in a cage. That he's free.

"I'm my own," he whispers.

I nod, smiling. He has such wonder in his eyes. We climb to our feet and go to each other. Our palms meet. His eyes are searching my face, his lips parted to say something. But the candles around us flicker. His hands suddenly go cold in mine then he jerks and pain flashes across his face.

The hair on the back of my arms and neck stands on end. She's entering him.

"Tristan, remember who you are," I say in a rush. "Fight. You're better than her."

His face is flushed and his fingers are digging into mine as he battles, but the sense of something growing around me is increasing. He is losing. Helping him focus on his past life helped him resist her before. But it won't work now. Because she was in his past.

Life is the present. I am the present. So I do the only thing I can think of to remind him of that. To leave her behind. I kiss him.

Chapter Seventeen

Tristan's lips are cold and taut against mine. His fingers are still digging into the backs of my hands. Then they relax. The world around me feels like it's spinning as he kisses me back. I feel her swirling around us. See the candles flickering wildly. So I close my eyes. My hair stops standing on end. She's growing weaker. Tristan lets go of one of my hands to slip his fingers into the hair at the base of my neck. He leans into me and his lips have grown warm. Hot.

I'm hot. She's gone.

I open my eyes and place my hand on his chest as I pull away. Resting my forehead on his, I can feel his breath panting against my wet lips, his pulse racing through our touching skin. There's a loud pop from my side and I jump. He grabs my arms, as if to shield me. But it was only the fire. We laugh. It's roaring even though we haven't done anything to tend it.

The candles and lamps are steady. Something tingling and light is spreading through my body from my chest. I rest my head against him and close my eyes as I feel his hand rest on the bare portion of my back. I can hear his heart beating.

"Is she gone?" I whisper.

When he speaks, his voice rumbles his throat. "She's weak. She's hiding."

"Good." I take a deep breath of his scent. Autumn leaves and iron blood. It's staining his clothing. With both his body heat and the fire, I'm too warm. But I don't move. He combs his fingers through my hair. I am at such peace.

We stay like that for some time. The longer he holds me and I hear his heart, the stronger I feel. This is a turning point, but not just against her.

I feel happy. Genuinely happy. Something I haven't felt since Scarlet died. I know that the darkness is still here, that our lives are still in danger, but right now I don't care. No, I do care. But I feel something more than that. Something stronger than my years of worry. Something blissful and addictive and intimidating. And I know I wouldn't be feeling it if not for him.

I tilt my head up to meet Tristan's eyes. He smiles at me and I trace my fingers down his jaw. His face is blooming. I'm blooming. He catches my hand in his and kisses each of my fingertips. I surprise myself when I realize I wouldn't mind his lips going anywhere on my body. The way he's looking at me makes me feel beautiful and I have no shame. I kiss his lips again.

Victoria can't use him against me anymore. I'm not taking him from her. He's taking himself from her. I'm just helping.

Grabbing his hand in mine, I lead him into the kitchen. I need to eat. While I finish off the rest of the smoked pork, I pretend I didn't just see Tristan eat a spider. I peer out the window, trying to see the sky. If she's weak, then maybe we've made some progress. If there has been any change, I can't see it.

We head back upstairs. If I couldn't get enough of Tristan's face before, I definitely can't now. It's radiating happiness, as is his body. His spirit. When he looks at me, I remember what sunlight feels like.

He stokes the fire to warm the chill out of the room. I spot my mother's wedding dress on the bed. Though it's tattered and torn and was never comfortable, it's more so than the gown I'm wearing now. And it never belonged to her. When Tristan sees that I mean to change, he pretends he is busy reading the titles of his books with his back to me.

I slip back into the old dress and fold the other up neatly. This one still has leaves and needles stuck on it but I don't mind. They remind me of how I got to this place. Of how much has changed.

I turn back to Tristan and find him leafing through his old journal. I can tell by the way his eyes are twitching back and forth that he's reading. He slowly sinks into the chair and I know he's forgotten that I'm here. Scarlet said that can happen sometimes. She said she used to get so absorbed in what she was reading that she would no longer be able to hear her surroundings. That can happen to me when I'm listening to a spirit whispering.

"What is it?" I ask, sitting down on the bed.

Tristan draws a breath, as if coming up for air after swimming. "My last journal entry."

I wait for him to continue but he doesn't. He goes back to reading. A line has formed between his brows. His body is taut. I wonder what the words could say to give him such focus. After some time, he shakes his head.

"It's the strangest thing... I can recall bits and pieces of my life, like the ones I've shown you. But I don't remember this day at all."

"Maybe it was unremarkable."

Tristan meets my gaze for a moment before holding up his journal. His voice shifts to sound a little monotonous and I realize he is reading to me. "Victoria slept in this morning. While she wouldn't notice my absence, I headed into the woods to procure herbs. I am hopeful this new remedy will be the one to cure her spells. Our supplies are running low. Improving her health enough to travel south is imperative if we are to remain here. Though I am hopeful that my new friend will be of some assistance. I stumbled upon him checking a snare this morning. His name is Lucian and he is a hunter by trade. He lives in the neighboring village."

"Morrot," I say, interrupting. Lucian was Draven's father, but Draven has never said anything to me about a house in the woods. Lucian must never have told him. I wave my hand. "Go on."

Tristan watches me for a few more moments, as if making sure I'm all right, then continues reading. "I spoke with him about trading medicine for supplies. The herbs I planted in Victoria's rose garden have done remarkably well so I have a ready store of treatments for common ails. As proof, I brought Lucian back home with me and made sure his game bag was well-stocked with vials and poultices before he was on his merry way.

"He has a gruff manner and is very to the point, but I like him. I think he and I shall be friends before long. He has even agreed to teach me to hunt, provided his village elder approves of our bartering. These mountain folk are strangely quiet but hearty. They seem to have very little contact with the world outside of their valley. I would very much like to spend time among them. Learn their ways. Perhaps even open a –" Tristan pauses. "Victoria." He closes the journal.

"What about her?"

"I scrawled her name. I must've stopped writing to see to her."

I nod, everything he just read trickling through my mind. If Lucian was young when he met Tristan, then this meeting was decades ago. However, if he was older, then this happened before the darkness when I was young. The idea that Tristan and I could've met in some other time and place has me spinning.

Would we have spoken? Would he have paid me any notice? Would we have been as drawn to each other as we are now?

There would still be the issue of Victoria. By the sound of his journal entry, he was looking for an escape from her even back then. For a friend. Or at the very least, a means to help his wife become a genuine companion.

Tristan carefully sets the journal down on the desk. "I wonder why I didn't write anymore after that day."

I'm about to ask if he died shortly after, but then I realize that's a silly question.

"I don't even recall what Lucian looked like," he says, his voice distant.

"He was tall," I say, drawing his attention. "With dirty blonde hair. A brown beard. Blue eyes."

"You know him?"

"Knew him."

Tristan crosses over to me and sits on the bed. He slips his hand around my waist. "Who was he?"

I lean my head against his shoulder. "He was my friend's father." Thinking of Draven is making me feel stiff inside. "He died over a year ago. Right around the same time Scarlet –"

We shouldn't be talking about her. It'll only make me sad. And resting against Tristan with my hand on his hip is reminding me of Draven and the woods and Lady's feather.

"Who is Scarlet?" he asks.

I feel a little sick and once again wonder if the pork was going bad. I wish it was that simple. I wish this anguish was something I could just gag and purge myself of. Something that I could leave ugly and foul on the ground and walk away from. But before I know it, I am speaking. "She was my sister," I whisper.

"Another *was*, not an *is*?"

I nod.

"A bigger was."

That does it. My face is contorting even before I feel the first cinch in my bruised throat or the first moisture in my eyes. I let out a dry sob. I try to make myself stop but after having cried so recently, it's as if the dam has already been broken. When I feel the heat of a tear gliding down my face I know that many more will follow. So many.

"I thought she was enchanted. She could do anything." Now my breath is hitching. "The best at dancing, singing, laughing. She made everyone laugh with her. Like magic. Then he said she was magic. Dark magic." My throat hurts so much now that I have to stop to take a shaky breath. His hands are on me, hugging me to him.

"Dark magic?" he asks. I feel his words in my hair, where his lips are.

I wipe at my cheek. "Elias, our village elder, taught her to read. She studied with him. He said he noticed a change in her. She read about sorcery in some of his books. She practiced witchcraft."

"What sort of witchcraft?" His warm breath is on my scalp.

"I never saw any. We never even got the chance to say goodbye."

"What happened?"

"I woke up one morning back when there was still some light in the sky. She was screaming. I ran and found her bound to a stake in the middle of the village. The hem of her dress was burning. She was burning. Draven held me back as she died. Elias said she was a witch, so he set her on fire."

Tristan's hands have gone still. He doesn't speak. I pull away to look at him. He has a peculiar expression on his face before he shakes his head, and his voice sounds distant again. "Burnt her?"

I can't stop the sob that bursts out. I can hardly talk around it. "I saw her die. And I couldn't stop it. They thought... they thought..."

But I can't speak anymore. Not coherently. I'm shaking and trying to breathe. I'm moving. It takes a moment to realize I'm lying down. Tristan is behind me, pulling my hair over my shoulder. I curl up and he rubs my bare arm.

It feels like tears and snot are leaking from everywhere. I can't get Scarlet's screams out of my head. The sight of her blackened, peeling feet. The stench of her burning hair. The sound of her laugh. The funny faces she'd make at me. The way we'd talk in exaggerated voices, imitating other villagers behind closed doors.

I cry so much that I have no memory of stopping. Only of waking. Time has passed. I know this because the room is nearly dark. The fire has burnt down low. One of my arms is cold but the back of me is warm and there is a weight on my waist.

Though I have been sleeping, my weeping has left me tired inside. That tiredness gives way to comfort as I realize Tristan is sleeping behind me. Usually I'm the one protecting Jasper. I didn't realize I was still bearing that weight until this moment. Until I felt someone else protecting me again like Scarlet did.

Twisting, I peer at him. Tristan's sound asleep. I can't make out much of his face in the dim light, but what I do is so endearing that I brush aside his hair and kiss his forehead. When I had set foot into the forest, headed for Sacrifice Rock, I never expected this. I never expected to find such belonging with a stranger. Such warmth amidst the chill of death. Such strength in whispers.

I roll over all the way and feel his soft breath against my chest. I'm still tired but for now I'm happy to just gaze at him. To let my eyes adjust enough to drink in his features. Were he graced with such beauty but had a cruel heart, I would only see the way his lips sort of frown. Instead, I see the way they dimple at the corners, looking like a reposed trouble-maker. I can't imagine that such a pleasant face, such a noble heart would find pleasure in me. A girl who once thought he was a creature. A monster.

The angle of Tristan's cheekbone is highlighted in silvery light. It suits him so well that it takes me a moment to recognize it. Silver light. Moonlight. The moon. Propping myself up on one elbow, I try to peer out the window. A mist in the air is glowing. I gently tug Tristan's arm off of my waist then tiptoe over to the sill.

I squeal at what I see. The beautiful, crescent moon. Clouds are streaking past but it has been so long since I've seen its light that I laugh. Tristan stirs behind me. I smile over my shoulder. "Come see." I hold out my hand.

He climbs out of bed and slips his fingers into mine. The moonlight hits his face in full and he grins.

"Oh, how glorious!" The mist churning in the forest below us appears enchanted. Like hoary dragon's breath or baby stars. "The darkness must be lifting."

Chapter Eighteen

I am so excited that I can't speak. I can only gawk like a fool and lean on the sill. Then I'm struck by a wild idea.

"Dance with me," I say. "Dance with me in the moonlight. Outside."

Tristan squeezes my hand. "I'll dance with you anywhere."

I gather up the hem of my mother's wedding dress and dart across the room. Tristan chuckles as he's yanked behind me. I know Victoria is weak because I can't even sense a spirit in this house other than Tristan's. Still, I pause at the top of the stairs, remembering how she tripped Tristan even when she didn't have a body.

The lamps downstairs burst to life. My heart races and I glance around. Where is she?

Then I spot Tristan's smile. He lit the lamps. She's not in control anymore. Tugging on my hand, he leads me down the stairs. We reach the front door and he tries the handle. It turns. I grin. I'm growing more and more certain that we've defeated her.

For the first time since I came to this place, I step outside. The air is moist and crisp, and the woods smell of damp mulch and smoke. I get goosebumps the moment the cold hits me. The house had been no warmer than the woods when I first arrived, but no longer.

I follow Tristan's gaze. He is standing on the stair below me while I'm on the top. At this height, our faces are level. The moon is a bright patch of cloud at the moment. But even the clouds are beautiful in its light. I am mesmerized by their swiftness. Their evanescence. I am reminded of spirits.

We descend the handful of steps. I am still barefoot and it takes a while to adjust to the icy wet beneath my feet. For the first time in months, I can see the branches of the dormant trees, coated in a sheen of moisture in the hoary light. The mist swirls slowly, clinging to the ground, surrounding us. Like we're in a cloud.

How beautiful the greens of new leaves will be as the ash and birch, beech and maple wake up. The thought makes me grab onto Tristan's arm, hugging it to my chest.

For some time we remain like that, side by side, watching the clouds glide over the moon. Then they thin and we glimpse the shadowed circle. I can see the freckles on its face. I count them. Then I am distracted by Tristan's fingers on my cheek.

He brushes aside a curl. I look at him and pause. His face is whitewashed but illuminated, as if he is glowing softly. We've never seen each other lit from above. I worry that he's taking in my gaunt cheeks. My pale skin. So pale that I'm likely to burn at the first touch of the sun.

"Always winter," he whispers. "At last it will be spring."

I smile and my lips tremble. I'll freeze if I don't move soon. Letting go of his arm, I snatch up his right hand and twirl beneath it. "One, two, three."

Tristan grins and catches me around the waist, falling into the box step again. "One, two, three."

Though my feet are numbing, my heart is light. We dance in a circle and the glittering mist parts around us. I twirl out away from Tristan, keeping one hand linked in his. He spins me back to him and I twist under his arm as the mist gyres. We move, making up the steps, falling into each other's rhythm. Then I begin one of our traditional dances.

Tristan follows my lead as I rest my forearms on his shoulders. He does the same to mine. It's a quick step. First in a circle one way, then back. Halfway back I peel away and pop my foot behind me. Tristan laughs then has to move quickly to catch up. We repeat the step, faster this time. Then I hold onto his waist and he holds onto mine. We turn in a circle one way then I twirl under his arm.

I laugh because he's watching my feet at first, worried he'll step on me. Maybe he has but I can't feel it. We repeat the steps, gaining speed like we used to do at the harvest festival. We'd spin faster and faster until there were only a few couples left. My blood is rushing through my veins, warming me against the night. Tristan's hand is growing damp. We dance until I have to catch my breath.

He slings his arms around my waist and I hook mine over his shoulders.

"Your dances are much more fun than mine," he says with a laugh. "Do you feel that?" He takes one of my hands and rests it on his heart. It's racing. So beautifully alive. He laughs again as he looks above my eyes. "You have moonlight in your hair."

I slip my hands under his vest and link them behind his back. My arms are warmed by his heat. I rest my head on his chest. His heart is slowing. He bends over me and I feel a gentle, pleasant pain on the side of my neck.

My bruises. He's kissing my bruises. One by one. I tilt my head back as he makes his way from one side to the other. I know it's not possible but I swear they feel better. At least, the sensation his lips are leaving behind feels better.

I know it was him who gave me the bruises in the first place. I'm trying to continue that thought. To somehow equate what he's doing to healing it. Making up for it. But that's not quite it. And I can't hold onto any thoughts anymore. They're leaving as soon as they enter. Enter what? Head. My head. I have a head. No, I don't. I only have a body and his lips are on it. Warmed by the tip of his tongue. By my ear. So hot when I'm so cold.

My eyes are shut. When did I close them? I don't care. My body is stiffening and softening at the same time. I'm getting warm again. A different sort of warm. A hungry sort. Only the hunger isn't in my belly. And heat is pooling in places I didn't think it could. My neck feels freezing when he pulls away. I open my eyes. I can't see his face because his temple is against mine. I've never been so aware of the curve of his body against me. Of his heat. Of my heat. I want to do something about it. I want him.

I press my fingertips into his back as I kiss him. My lips have never felt like this before. Such teasing pleasure. I need more of it. And so does he. His hands are in my hair, on my backside, on my thighs. I try to keep track of them. They feel like there's more than two. But his lips are intoxicating, so warm like his tongue.

This is why we have bodies. To make love.

His vest is gone. I'm unbuttoning his shirt. Who has this many buttons, anyway? I try not to tear them but my hands are shaking, because his are on my backside, pressing me to him. His lips and tongue are on the side of my neck. I fumble with the last button and can't undo it. He's distracting me. I think my skin is stretching, reaching for him. I slide my fingers up his back. Smooth skin and taut muscle. Warmth. I tangle my other in his hair. His scalp is sticky, moist with sweat.

I catch his lips with mine. He lets go of me to cup my face. We're both panting so much that we shouldn't be kissing but we are. I can't stop. My hand is yanking on his trousers before I know it. Anticipation blooms inside when my knuckles brush his firm abdomen. His breath hitches as my hand slides to the clasp. Then the heat is gone. It fades so quickly that I blink and stagger.

He has yanked away from me. His back is turned. His shoulders slumped. My skin is hungry for his. I try to calm it down but I can't. And then it's as if I can think again for the first time. Being unable to quiet my physical senses has never happened before. I could always still them enough to listen if I tried. Unless I was in danger.

This is no danger. This is different. My eyes are on his backside. I want it. This is lust.

I want to go to him but I don't trust myself. I'll try to kindle the fire all over again. My blood is hungry to make his race once more. So instead I force myself to stand there. To let the cold seep in. My lips are throbbing with my pulse. It takes more willpower than I ever thought, but I stay where I am. I can feel the sweat on my body as it starts to cool.

Tristan remains where he stopped several paces away, unmoving. As my skin cools and I can think again, I think too much. Have I upset him? Does he not want me like I want him? Of course he doesn't. I'm too skinny. I'm not all that pretty. But I pleased him. Didn't I please him? I have no experience. I've done something wrong.

I blush. The heat in my face only increases when I retrace my steps. I've never wanted someone to touch me like that before. I've never wanted to touch someone like that before.

He shifts his weight then looks at me over his shoulder, biting his lower lip. I force myself not to take notice of how seductively innocent the expression on his face is. How he's drawing attention to his lips. How the moonlight is pooling in his eyes, making them appear larger than they are. I fail.

"You're very beautiful," he says quietly. "Inside and out."

He steps back over to me and I feel myself stiffen. My heart starts to flutter in advance and I tell it to calm down to soothe my blood. He pauses before me. There's no use trying to avoid the nakedness of his chest. Slender muscles kissed by the moon. A thin scar from the bounty hunter. He rests his palm against my cheek, his fingers slipping into the hair on my temple. Our foreheads touch. I close my eyes when he speaks because his voice has become so dear to me.

"But we are more than just bodies."

"This is why we have them," I say. I'm surprised by the pouty tone in my voice.

Tristan combs his fingers through the drying sweat in my hair then kisses me. His lips are cool and dry. The fire is gone. "I want to see the sunrise," he whispers.

I nod. Disappointment is quickly slithering through me. I don't understand why being more than bodies means we shouldn't use them. Shouldn't enjoy them. I've been distracted by my thoughts. He has stepped away from me and buttoned his shirt back up.

"Let's go inside where it's warm."

I take a deep breath then slowly let it out. I shouldn't be embarrassed. I shouldn't be disappointed. He doesn't seem to think any less of me. He's holding his hand out for mine. As I take it, I feel something solidify in my chest again. *Trust*. I have always trusted him. Maybe he was worried that our desire would break that trust. Would result in something we'd regret. I can't see myself regretting it, but maybe he knows something that I don't.

We head back inside and up to our room. He stokes the fire again and my skin begins to thaw. I hadn't realized how cold I was. My feet hurt a little as they warm up. Tristan hugs me from behind as we lie down. He kisses the back of my neck. It stirs an echo of hunger but nothing more. We're facing the window this time. The moon has shifted and is no longer in sight. Tristan sighs, making my hair tickle my back.

The warmth of the room and his body are making me sleepy. Lying here now, I am so comfortable that I am grateful that nothing was ruined. I am grateful that I still feel safe. That I can still lie beside him and not think of him as just a body. But it's not his body that I want on its own. I only want it because it's his. I hope he knows that.

I feel a brush of shame when I think of how eager I was to have him. I wanted him inside of me. And then it hits me. Inside of me. Victoria. He stopped himself because of Victoria. Did my passion remind him of hers? Did I hurt him like she did? Or maybe it's how quickly this has all come about that made him want to slow down. How much things have changed. How quickly he has changed. He turned on a dime for Victoria. She was a mistake. I'm not a mistake. Am I?

My thoughts circle. Tristan's breathing is steady behind me. The moonlight is gone. It's dark outside. The sun isn't coming up. It isn't coming up because we haven't won after all. He stopped himself tonight for the same reason the darkness hasn't left. He's still loyal to his wife. As long as they are bound together, the darkness will remain.

How could he still be loyal to Victoria, after all he has shown me and all we have shared? How could he still need her? He was so happy to be rid of her, to be his own man. Though I suppose such bonds of love and madness are not easily broken. I should've known better.

I somehow manage to fall asleep. I wake up from Tristan stirring. He has a smile on his face when I roll over to look at him.

"Hello," he says.

His simple greeting reminds me of how far he has come. I remember last night and am glad that we didn't change things. Whatever his lingering feelings are for Victoria, I also know he's not ready for complicated yet. And neither am I. "Hello," I reply with a smile.

Tristan's face turns grave. "I was hoping for sun."

I sigh and rub my eyes before sitting up. I try to think of how to tell him that he has to let her go. He's looking at me like he knows I'm going to say something. His eyes search mine as he waits. But when I part my lips to speak, there's a noise downstairs.

We both leap off the bed. My ankle twinges. Tristan makes sure the key is in the lock. It is. He sags in relief. We still and hold our breath, listening.

Tapping. Something downstairs is tapping. Against a wall. Like a door that's been flung open. Tristan and I look at each other. His confusion matches mine. She isn't as weak as we thought. Then the front door closes. It's an unmistakable sound. I narrow my eyes. This is a new trick of hers.

Light footsteps echo in the parlor. Heel toe. Heel toe. Soft tread. Cautious movement. I know that sound. But before I can place it, I'm yanking on the key and opening the door. Tristan grabs my arm to stop me but I brush past him. He's at my side as I lean over the railing, peering down into the near darkness.

The figure below has heard us and stopped moving. It takes a moment for my eyes to adjust to the dimness downstairs. The embers are only giving off a glow but it's enough. Standing in the parlor, his crossbow aimed at us, is Draven.

Chapter Nineteen

Tristan sees the weapon at the same time I do. He yanks me behind him.

"Draven," I shout. Tristan is backing up to our room. He's trying to protect me but I don't need protecting.

Draven's voice sounds shocked. "Willow?"

"Don't shoot," I yell, even as I hear his boots on the stairs, running up. Tristan's gripping my arm, using his body as a shield. One of the lamps on the wall in the hall bursts to life. I'm used to the light in our room, but Draven isn't. He stumbles at the top of the stairs, squinting and raising a hand to shield his eyes, his crossbow limp at his side.

"It's all right," I whisper to Tristan in a rush as I step past him. He lets me go. I grab onto Draven in a hug.

Draven flutters out of my arms. Backing away, he looks me up and down. His eyes are wide. They keep darting all over my body. They settle on the bruises on my neck and he takes a half-step forward then stops.

"You're hurt," he mutters. I don't realize I've missed the deepness of his voice until I hear it. Then he meets my gaze. "You're alive."

Now I understand his flightiness. I wonder how long I've been gone. How long they've thought me dead.

Draven cocks his head. "Alive?" he whispers.

I nod and smile. He tentatively holds out a hand, reaching to touch me. Tristan rests a hand on my back and I can feel his tension grow.

Draven's boots quietly slide forward, his broad shoulders taut, as if ready to leap back if I bite. The orange lamplight is pooling in his eyes. Like hearths. I think he's reaching for my face but instead he touches a curl framing it and fingers it between his dirty forefinger and thumb. Then we both smile. As if given something we thought lost. He hugs me back this time, and I am engulfed in leather and pine.

"What're you doing here?" I ask. "How's my family?"

"Hungry but alive." He pulls away.

"They think I'm dead?"

He nods, his expression solemn though his eyes are still dancing all over me.

"Hello," Tristan says from behind me. Though his tone is friendly, he's watching Draven like a cat watches a bird.

Draven inclines his head. "Draven."

Tristan doesn't answer. His lips are growing taut, his eyes boring into Draven's, his body tense. I'm about to introduce Tristan for him when blood blooms on his right shoulder. Then I remember. Draven shot him once. Tristan looks ready to pounce at the slightest provocation. And though Draven may appear outwardly calm, I know his hand is not idly holding his crossbow as he seems.

I step between the two.

"Tristan," he says at last, his voice strained.

Draven's eyes settle on mine, asking for an explanation. I hold his gaze for a few moments longer. *Later*. He blinks and I know he understands.

"What're you doing here?" I ask.

"You ought to have knocked," Tristan snips.

I arch a brow at him and he relaxes his stance, folding his hands in front of him. Not as friendly as a man as he was as a spirit. Then again, he has reason to be wary of the boy with the bow.

Draven sucks in a breath and hooks his crossbow onto his belt, shifting his weight as he relaxes. "Following a deer."

"A deer?" They're scarcer than rabbits.

"Sounded like a deer. It led me here." He glances around the illuminated hallway. I remember my first impressions of this house. Such grandeur. "Do you live here?"

"Yes," Tristan says, stepping up to my side.

Draven's brows lower over his dark eyes. "How've you survived? Game this deep in died first."

"I didn't," Tristan replies.

Draven's eyes flick over Tristan's refined clothing. Tristan doesn't offer any more information. Draven looks to me, his jaw set. "If there's food to be had, then I must know. Elias is starting a lottery."

"What kind of lottery?" I ask.

"One where the winner is butchered."

It takes a few moments for his meaning to make sense. Cannibalism. Morrot is going to devour itself. Has it really come to this?

"The name will be drawn tomorrow," Draven says.

That's why he was so deep in the woods. So recklessly searching for any game.

"So I ask again. Is there any food to be had?"

Tristan's eyes have softened. He shakes his head. "No."

Draven's shoulders tense. He takes in the slightest breath and holds it. It's enough to tell me how disappointed he is. How hopeful he'd been when he found the house. We need to catch whatever it was he was hunting. Something to stave the hunger. I don't want to think of my parents' names being drawn. Or anyone's, for that matter. Least of all consuming the flesh of your neighbor. He had said a deer led him here. Led him. A chill jets down my spine. That was no deer.

"You have to go," I say breathlessly.

"What?"

Tristan steps closer to me. "It was her," I whisper to him. "In the woods."

"Get out," Tristan hisses, brushing past me.

Draven takes a step back. His eyes flit between Tristan and me.

Tristan points to the door downstairs. Draven blinks, as if clearing his vision, then steps forward, holding his hand out for mine.

I stare at it. His fingernails are stained and chipped and a scar is peeking out from under his sleeve. A thin white line as a reminder of Lady's claws. He presses his lips together. I feel my hand twitch but I keep it at my side. Tristan's back is stiffening.

"Willow?" Draven whispers.

I part my lips but no words come. I want to see my family again. I want to smell Jasper's hair. But I can't go. I can't abandon Tristan. Even if he is growing taut, like he wants to strike. More man right now than I'd prefer. He still needs me to guide him. To protect him. I shake my head.

Draven lets his hand fall to his side. He looks at Tristan with a gaze both sad and cunning. He has seen the change in me. He knows how I feel. For a moment, I'm worried he'll lash out. Then the same look crosses his face that did when he first saw me after his father died.

When his gaze briefly meets mine, I feel an ache in my chest. Like the twisting of the roots his constant presence has grown in my life. No matter what happens now, I know those roots will wither and die.

The leather of Draven's trousers creaks as he steps back.

"Go," Tristan says lowly.

Draven shuffles to the top of the stair. He rests his hand on the railing then pauses. I'm having trouble breathing steadily. He casts me one last look over his shoulder. Our roots are already growing cold. I'm growing cold. He hurries down the stairs. Then I realize I'm not cold, after all. My hair is standing on end. But I've noticed too late.

I suck in a lungful of air. Draven's boots echo in the entryway. I scream his name just as a black, shrouded form flies into him from the dining room.

Tristan grabs my arm and yanks. I hear Draven go down. The lamp above my head shatters. The oil burns radiantly for a moment, and I glimpse Victoria's corpse on top of Draven and Tristan's shoulder as he pushes me. Then the oil burns out completely. Darkness surrounds me until Tristan shoves me into the bedroom.

He slams the door before locking it.

"Draven!" I try to shove Tristan out of the way but he grabs my shoulders. "You can't leave him out there!"

"Stay here," Tristan hisses. "I'll –"

He gags. That horrible gag when Victoria summons him. No, she can't have him, too.

"She can't hurt you," I say in a rush, resting my hand on the side of his face. "You're your own, remember?"

"You don't understand," Tristan gasps. "It's my fault."

He isn't making sense but he's in pain. I kiss him. He lets out another choking sound. My kiss hasn't calmed him. Why hasn't it calmed him? Because of his loyalty to that decrepit woman. What is she doing to Draven? I can hear him screaming.

"She's *dead*, Tristan. You owe her nothing!"

"I owe her everything," he snaps then gags.

His expression is strained. Each breath is a struggle. I'm about to shove him aside and go after Draven myself when his fingers dig into my shoulder.

"There is something about me you don't know," he gasps. "Something you need to know before I..."

Tristan coughs and doubles over. I try to catch him. He touches my face. Whispers build around me in my mind. I don't want this. Not now.

Draven. I have to help Draven. But Tristan's forehead is touching mine. Daylight invades my senses as I'm yanked into his memory once more.

I'm downstairs in the kitchen while Victoria is shrieking in the bedroom. I'm attempting to mix something green with a mortar and pestle but it's hard with the pain. My hands are shaking like a rheumatic's. The skin of my arms is black and blistering red and I know my back is just as damaged. I can't even wear a shirt. Victoria lets out another shriek and sounds like an animal. She has screamed so much that she spit out blood. That's why I'm here.

I scrape the green mash into a glass and stir it. This will help her throat. I move away from the counter but twist too quickly. I cry out in pain and drop the glass and it shatters on the floor. That was the last of the nettles that numb. That was the last remedy that could dull her pain. Tears are blurring my vision as despair takes hold of me.

Can't I do anything to help my wife? Victoria screams out my name. Had she not been screaming it earlier, I would never have recognized it amidst her tormented sounds.

While I'm bent over, I vomit. It's white foam. I can't recall the last time I ate. I can't even contemplate food. I gasp as I straighten. My back feels like it's getting burned all over again. I have existed in such agony since that horrible day that I don't see how I could ever recover. I'm wheezing again so I take a moment to catch my breath.

"Tristan," she shrieks then gurgles and I worry she is choking on her own blood.

I force myself to move and climb the stairs. I have to hold onto the railing because I'm still shaking so much. Hoisting my weight up each step feels like the skin on my back is cracking. Perhaps it is. I'm so winded and dizzy at the top of the stairs that I gag. I dry heave but nothing comes out other than acid eating away at my lips. Victoria's shrieking has subsided to moaning.

The door at the end of the hall is open. I can glimpse her dark form on the bed, bathed in daylight from the burnt out wall.

Placing one foot in front of the other, I limp down the hall. Victoria is whimpering and moaning. The shock of seeing her like this hits me anew even though she has been this way for days. We both have. Her body is covered in burns. More than half of her face is black and peeling and oozing blood as it dies. I can see one of her teeth through a charred hole. Her eye is dark red mush, like a bruised plumb. The dress she was wearing when the fire caught her is attached to her, melted in place by her skin. It hides the scaly, puss-filled burns on the rest of her body.

I want to be sick again but I can't. I am empty and the room is spinning for a moment. I don't want to lose consciousness again. Last time that happened, I couldn't get up without passing back out from the pain. It took me far too many attempts.

"Victoria," I whisper.

She groans in response. Blood is trickling out of her mouth, staining the pillow with the rest of her soot and rot. I don't know how to tell her that I dropped her medicine which was the one thing that could ease her suffering. I gently sit on the bed beside her.

"Tristan," she mumbles.

It sounds like her tongue has become so swollen that she can no longer move it. Her lips are falling off. She groans and tenses. She starts thrashing. Watery blood leaks from her dead eye. She can't take much more writhing but she can't control it, either. I know it hurts her, but I rest my palms on either of her shoulders to still her. Victoria shrieks at the contact but it limits her seizing.

Blood rushes out of her mouth, bubbling with spittle. Her blackened arms jerk up as she convulses. That hasn't happened before. I wonder if that means this will be the last and she will finally be out of her suffering.

Then I'm being burned again. My scream is twining with hers. I feel the flames on my arms digging into my flesh anew. However looking down, I see that there's no fire. It is her hands digging into my charred skin. Her yellowed fingernails carving twisted trails down my forearms as she convulses. My head doesn't feel attached anymore. The pain is so much that my hearing dims. I'm only aware that I'm screaming because I can feel it in my throat.

When I am able to see again, Victoria is still. I release her. Blood is pouring down my arms. Her good eye swivels in its socket as she studies me. She is holding something. A knife.

Where did she get it? Yes, I brought it up here to cut away parts of her dress weeks ago. Only it wasn't weeks. It can't have been weeks for there have only been three nights.

"Take it," she wheezes.

My hands have gone numb. The pinkness of their unburned skin, though slick with rivulets of blood, makes it look like I'm wearing gory sleeves. I manage to grasp the hilt of the blade.

"Kill me," she wheezes then lets out a whimper.

I shake my head.

"Kill me, or I'll kill you."

It's an idle threat and we both know it. She can't even sit up. Her eye swivels to my arm as I raise it, testing my motion.

"Oh, Tristan," she hisses. She coughs out more blood and spittle, as if she couldn't be any more wretched. "Your body. Your beautiful body..."

"Just rest," I say. I'm getting dizzy again and I won't be able to stay conscious much longer. I'll be of no use to her once I black out. "Rest..." I slur.

I close my eyes. It feels like the house is spinning. Then I smell burnt flesh and feel her cold, crisp hand on my cheek. I open my eyes.

"Can't feel your skin," she wheezes. Of course she can't. The poor thing barely has the fingertips to even touch me. "Tristan... kill me."

I shake my head. Her body tenses again with another seizure.

"Kill me," she gurgles loudly.

"I can't." Tears blur my vision as she starts to convulse. Boiling sounds come from her throat. She's hemorrhaging. "Victoria, I'm so sorry."

"Kill," she wheezes.

Blood and spittle fly out of her mouth as she clears her throat, making way for screams. She shrieks. My ears are ringing. She chokes as a piece of her throat temporarily clogs her windpipe. Half my vision is red. Blood is pouring down my face. She's clawing it off.

My arm moves. Her screaming stops. She goes still. Blood trickles from the gash in her neck and the side of my face. I drop the knife.

I've just killed my wife.

Then I tear inside. A pain worse than burning. Something heavy moves through me and when it's gone, I am left with a lighter body than before. As if gravity has become less severe. The pain is now tolerable. This is more than relief that my wife is no longer suffering. My physical senses have dulled. Am I dying?

Now I'm slumped on her grave with the scent of fresh dirt

staining my hands. My healing arms are searing as my skin cracks. I'll have to wait before I even try to make a headstone. Wait until I can move again for my back is stinging awfully. My wounds should be infected by now, but somehow I manage to get through each day, healing a little more than the last.

A cloud drifts past the sun and I wonder if it will rain. I glance upwards to see if there are more but there are no clouds at all. Instead there is a dark haze like thin smoke. I wonder what that could be.

The whispers fade and I'm brought back into the present. I jerk away from Tristan and vomit. My senses are still ringing from the pain. Dulled by the screams. I fall over and narrowly avoid my puddle of sick. My body isn't working right now. Tristan's horrible memory is still staining me like smoke.

He's whimpering nearby. I work my jaw and get my ears to pop, but I am dizzy. And through it all, I hear Draven screaming my name. Then Tristan is screaming. Those horrible sounds when his life is being wrenched from him. Because he's giving up. He's letting her take. I've had too many screams. I cover my ears and curl up.

Chapter Twenty

The house is silent. I pull my hands away from my ears. I don't know what happened to me. Dried tears are on my cheeks. My vomit is stinking a foot away. I've had enough. I had enough. I shut down for a while. I guess I played dead. I wipe any lingering bile off my lips. For a moment, I remember doing so as Tristan. But I'm not Tristan. That memory wasn't mine. I killed Victoria. No. *Tristan*. Tristan killed Victoria. It's him who's trapped in a prison of fire and pain. Not me.

Then who am I? Willow? No, that's just a name. It doesn't mean anything. Just a word people call me. I find that funny. I don't know who I am. Am I dead? Is this the Netherworld? Was I really killed at Sacrifice Rock? The stench of my vomit and my headache remind me that I am alive. I'm alone in the room.

I am worse than dead. I am mad. Tristan is mad. This house is mad. I think I've been half-crazy all along. Hearing the voices of the dead. Why couldn't Scarlet hear them? Why couldn't my mother? Only my grandmother. I wonder if she knew who she was as she fell. Was she just a name? An empty vessel for spirits to fill with their needs?

Why do I even bother to eat or drink? We all end up the same way. Alone. Dead. Simpletons.

I look at the door. It's still locked. Why was it locked? To keep her out?

Draven.

Where is Draven? I shove myself up and feel nauseated again. Tristan... He doesn't have a body anymore. Did he ever? Was Draven really here? Did I imagine him?

I creep over to the door and listen. Nothing. No lights. I turn the key and open the door. It creaks as it moves. It's shoving something. Broken glass. The lamp.

"Draven?" I call. There is no answer.

Holding onto the railing, I head down the stairs one at a time. I know this is dangerous but I don't think she can do much more to hurt me. Not with how I'm feeling right now. In the parlor, I use a burning twig to light a lamp. How these candles and lamps never run low, I don't know. It's all part of the madness. All part of the nonsense that is death. The unraveling of rules. The breaking of barriers.

This room is empty. I bite my lip. What was I looking for? Why don't I just leave?

The boy with the falcon. Yes, that's who. He's important to me. I see Lady's face in my head and I stiffen. I feel like I'm waking up. Like I'm shrugging off the darkness and shadows and memories that have confused me into thinking that I'm not me. I am me. I am light. Tristan said it.

My heart begins to race. I don't know how much time has passed. Draven was alone with her as she gained strength. I remember what she did to me with the pearls. Where is he?

I run into the dining room. Nothing. I check the kitchen. Empty. I'm about to run back and check upstairs when I notice a drop of blood on the ground. It's shiny. It's new.

Then I see another. And another. There's a trail. Hurrying after them, I find myself at the front door. I step outside. The crescent moon is back. Cold flakes melt against my bare arms and face. It's snowing, but only lightly. In the lamplight, I can see that it hasn't even stuck to the ground yet. Which is good, because if I look very carefully, I can see more drops of blood. Like rubies. Cold slips up the slit in my dress and numbs my feet.

It's taking too long to hunt each drop down. I round a corner. He's out here somewhere. Picking my way forward, I reach the back of the house. A spiked metal fence encompasses what I can only imagine was once Victoria's rose garden. I follow the fence to a small gate and shove. The bushes are dead and black but still standing. The only spot of color is across from me. A solitary red rose, vibrant even from here.

As I step towards the rose, I notice a dark form below it. I know those long legs. I run.

Draven is slumped against a slab of rock. His hands are bound just above his head, to what I realize is a tombstone. Chains wrap around his torso, lashing him to the rock on top of Victoria's grave. I set down the lamp and kneel beside him, touching his face. He's breathing but cold. Too cold.

He opens his eyes at my touch. I want to hug him to make him warmer but I see no way to undo the chains. He blinks dazedly and as he lifts his head, I see why. There is a hole in the side of his neck. Glistening dark. Like someone chewed on him. I don't want to hold the light any closer to the wound. I don't want to see how bad it is.

"Draven..."

Something drips onto my hand. Blood. I look up and find the blooming rose glistening. It's been painted red with Draven's blood.

"Don't you like it?" The sing-song voice startles me.

I whip my head around to spot none other than Victoria slinking out of the shadows. The shock of it makes me fall on my backside. The lamp is snuffed out.

In the moonlight, she looks just as she did in life. Only fading. As if her colors and features are being filled in as fast as they're dissolving. She's still in her funerary shrouds, only she holds up the hem like a dress and has her veil over her hair, not her face. As if she was some ghoulish bride. She wipes blood off of her chin.

"I've always preferred red roses."

She's speaking to me. Not with whispers, but with her voice.

Victoria died. I watched her. I felt Tristan's hand move as he did it. Yet she licks the blood off the back of her hand then leans against her tombstone. Leans. She can only lean if she has a body.

Victoria arches a brow then looks down on herself. She holds up a piece of her shrouds, revealing too much thigh.

"What, this?" She lets it fall back onto place then crosses her wrists in front of her, leaning on her forearms as if we were gossiping.

"I have you to thank for it. You gave my husband back his strength. His confidence. Just when I was growing so weak. You built him up enough so that when I fed, I could get this back." She grabs her breasts. "I owe you such thanks." Her expression darkens. "I'd give it to you if you weren't a little whore."

My lungs are growing cold as I pant.

Draven is now conscious enough to struggle. He winces as he tries to free his wrists. Victoria is smirking as she watches him. Then she saunters over.

"Not a bad looking boy. A little skinny." She grabs Draven by the hair and yanks his head back, causing him to cry out. "Is he yours?"

I narrow my eyes at her. I'm clenching my fists. My heart is racing. I regret not grabbing a weapon when I had the chance. But I never thought I'd face this.

She raises her brows. "No? Well then." She straddles Draven. "Then you won't mind me," she simpers as she sits on him. She still has his head yanked at an angle and throws me a taunting look, as if this is some sort of revenge. "Or will you?"

With a freakish jerk, she tilts her head to the side and clamps down on the hole she's already made in his neck. Draven screams. This *is* revenge. For touching her husband. For picking her rose without permission.

Something in me snaps. Like a flame bursting to life. I scream and leap. My shoulders ram into hers as I knock her aside. Her thin body lands beneath mine with a thump. I sit up to grab her neck then my knees hit the ground. She has disappeared.

A chuckle rises from behind me. I twist about. She's there, licking the blood off her lips as she shakes with amusement. Draven is kicking as he squirms, trying to get out of the chains, his neck slick with blood. I don't know what Victoria has become, but I know she'll only slip away again if I try to harm the body she worked so hard to restore.

I grab onto Draven's chains and yank. They only grow tighter. He yelps as his chest is constricted. I feel their lengths, hunting for their ends. There are none. How is this possible?

"What truths?" Victoria asks. "What laws of the earth exist after death?"

The chains around Draven yank and he squeaks. He can't breathe. She's controlling them.

"The living surround themselves with barriers but what do you really know about your world?"

She's stepping closer to me. I'm on my knees, yanking on Draven's chains. They're so cold. He's screwing his eyes shut. Victoria's voice sounds like my mind. The torment of a Listener. The torment of knowing that she's right.

"Can you really trust anything?" she whispers in my ear.

I stop yanking. Draven's throat is hissing, like he's only getting thimblefuls of air. She's right. No one can trust anything. Nothing's stable. Nothing's as it seems. I'm just a vessel. A name.

Victoria rests a cold hand on my shoulder. "That's why we must take what we can while we can. There's no point in giving back. Beauty is for the beholder."

Chilling wind cuts through my hair, peppering me with snowflakes. It's tearing up my eyes so I close them.

Tristan is hers. Now she is claiming me, as well.

We must take while we can because nothing is steadfast. Take, take, take. The back of my brain is burning. It's tearing apart at the seams. I can't hear Draven breathing anymore. Neither can I stop him from dying. I can't stop anyone from dying. We all die. We all are forgotten. We all lose sense in the Netherworld. Bumbling simpletons who walk down hallways every night.

Even the most vibrant among us diminish. Even Scarlet. Big sisters aren't supposed to leave. But she did. She's never coming back.

I can't change that. I can't change anything. I am powerless. Fighting is no use. Living is so hard when we're all dying. From the first breath we take. Much easier to give in. To live in darkness.

Then I hear it. A whisper like wind in the trees on a summer's night. Playful and dancing. There's a weight on my other shoulder. Like a hand only without any pressure. My eyes are stilled closed. Victoria is on my right, wooing me. But I don't need to open my eyes to know that my sister is on my left. Warmth spreads through me like sunlight. She's hugging me. I smell apples. I smell Scarlet.

"I would've danced at your wedding," she whispers in my mind. I can hear her voice clear as day. Or dark as night. "You must dance for me."

I lean to the left. The scent of apples intensifies. I couldn't save her. I watched her die. So much darkness. I am like Victoria. I want Scarlet to fill me. To live with her presence at my side forever.

"I am always with you," she says. "And I am so proud of you. You're my sister. You're my sister. I love you."

Scarlet is filling me with warmth. With blossoming strength. She's filling me with something greater than the cold. Deeper than the darkness. It's what made her laugh contagious. What made her eyes sparkle. What made her so enchanting. Love. Love so freely-given and unwavering that she wore it like magic.

I open my eyes. Victoria's funerary shrouds flutter beside me. Something twinges in my mind. Something important from Scarlet to unfold later. Draven is fighting. His lips are blue, he can barely breathe, and blood is pulsing from the wound in his neck. But he is fighting. His dark eyes are fixed on me. And in them I see hearths. And I know that Victoria is wrong.

I am no empty vessel. I am not just a name. I am a sister. I am loved. Loved is me.

I can feel Scarlet smiling. I can see her face in my mind. The chains in my hands are cold like Victoria. Though wind is still cutting across my face, hurting my eyes, I don't blink as I gaze into Draven's eyes.

"I will not take," I gasp. Victoria's hand on my shoulder tightens. I let go of the chains and grab Draven's limp hand. "I will gather. I will receive. And I will give. I will give so much."

Scarlet's strength is now burning inside me. Like a whirlwind. Victoria's fingernails are drawing blood as I slowly look up to her. I may be young, but I'm not Tristan. I'm not hungry for acceptance. I already have it. I am not hers.

"And you," I snarl, rising to my feet. Victoria sneers as my head becomes level with hers. "Will go to the Netherworld where you belong."

Victoria's face twists as her grip turns to ice. She parts her blood-caked lips and screams. She raises her hand to slap me. The chains yank tight around Draven, killing him.

I feel Scarlet flare then leave me. Burning like heat, she is white light, tearing through Victoria. Her scream ends as both her body and Scarlet's light disappear. The chains around Draven thud as they fall to the ground. He wheezes, so desperate for air that he's arching against the tombstone.

I fall to my knees beside him, resting a hand on his shoulder and another on the side of his face as he struggles to force air into his aching lungs. His skin is cold and his stubble prickles my palm. His eyes are so fixed and dull in the moonlight that I'm worried I'm too late. He's fading. Then he blinks and they regain their glow. He rests his hand on mine against his face, gasping.

Something falls off my cheek. A tear. I'm crying. I slump beside Draven and hug him to my chest. I rest my chin on his hair and can feel his ribs rising and falling as they bellow life back into his blood. He'll be all right. He just needs more air.

Draven grabs the collar of my dress, his arm trembling. Holding on as if I am life. I hold him tighter as he quivers. The breeze is chilling me but I don't dare let go.

I don't know what happened to Victoria. How long it will take for her to lick her wounds. But Scarlet has given me time. She has given me Draven. And something else.

I watch the moon through the dead branches. They look like they're reaching for the sky, like twisted, pleading worshippers.

Followers. Sheep. We have all been sheep following Elias. Scarlet's message unfolds in my mind. She has shown me the truth. Planted the knowledge as if she told it to me in person.

Elias knew she wasn't a witch. He knew she wasn't practicing dark magic. Yet still, she had bewitched him. He was drawn to the wit of her quick mind. She was his challenge. He tried to charm her. He let her read books he loaned to no one else. He complimented her beauty.

He made her uncomfortable. Unsafe. She started avoiding him. Until one evening, while tidying up after her studies, something fell out of a book. It was a feather. Assuming it was a bookmark, she opened the tome back up to the dented page. The feather had been attached to a necklace. A necklace of falcon feathers that Draven had made for Lucian.

Elias found her looking at the keepsake. She didn't ask for an explanation but he gave one anyway. He told a story about a house Lucian had found in the woods. A house with a young apothecary who wanted to bring the modern world into our valley. So he poured resin into the chimney of one of the apothecary's fireplaces. It burst in an explosion of flame when lit. Elias had seen the black smoke from the village and knew the threat was removed. Lucian was the only other villager who understood what the smoke meant.

The darkness began shortly after. Lucian told Elias that we should seek help from elsewhere before it was too late. But Elias refused, even if it meant living in darkness. He surprised Lucian when he was checking a trap in the woods. He shoved him down a slope to his death.

Thus, no one ever found out about the house in the woods and the outside world it came from. No one except for Scarlet. She tried to flee but Elias stopped her. He forced her into his bed but she would have none of it. He claimed only a witch could make him confess like he did. Only a witch would deny her leader her love.

That was the night he lashed her to the stake. The morning that we awoke to her screams. He didn't only kill my sister. We've been following a mass murderer.

Chapter Twenty-One

The moonlight is veiled with cloud. I feel like a statue in this graveyard. My joints are locked around Draven in the cold. His chest is no longer heaving, his windpipe no longer wheezing. I worry he has passed out again. His wound needs to be bound. How did we all become pawns? Even Victoria. Elias has caused all of this. Him and his lust for control.

Greed: the true Bringer of Darkness.

"Willow?" Draven whispers. His voice is hoarse and weak, but it'll do.

I shift my weight to let him know I heard him. I should speak but if I do, I'll tell him everything. He deserves to know. But not yet.

"Ribs are broken."

I nod. Moving slowly, which is easy since I'm stiff from the cold, I untangle myself. Once on my feet, I help him up. He screws his eyes shut as he forces himself off the ground. I pull one of his arms over my shoulders and wait until he is steady before I take a step. The snow is still falling. It's starting to stick to the ground.

Slowly, we make our way back to the house. Once inside, I help Draven sit in one of the armchairs in the parlor then stoke the fire. I fetch us both some water. Yet even as I do so, I am listening. Victoria isn't gone. She's still dangerous. I wonder where Tristan is. How long it will take until I can see him again. I raid the linen closet and tear up a clean cloth.

Kneeling beside Draven, I'm forced to look at the wound. The flesh around the hole is jagged and white. Blood is still draining but from what I can tell, nothing critical is exposed. Only small veins. I pack it with linen then wind a strip around his neck, holding the dressing in place. I'm no healer. I've never done something like this before. But I figure it's better than leaving it open and leaking. He needs that blood. Too much is staining the shoulder and chest of his tunic.

When I straighten, I find Draven's face tight and beads of sweat on his brow. I wish there were more I could do for him. His skin is thawing and he looks a little better. Stable. I hand him a goblet of water and he tries to hand it back.

"You need to drink," I say.

Was he anyone other than Draven, I'd be surprised that he wasn't bombarding me with questions. Demanding explanations. Accusing me of deceit. Instead, he seems content to wait. Not out of a desire for ignorance, but out of patience. Trust.

He sips his water. I sit on the hearth. Words are building inside me. Words I need to share. I hope Tristan is near. I hope he can hear me. This is for him, as well.

"Draven..."

He watches me through half-lidded eyes. His head leans against the back of the chair. I'm worried he'll fall asleep.

"Your father's death wasn't an accident. He was killed. By Elias."

Draven's eyes open a bit more. Though I know it must hurt him, he tries to sit up straighter.

"Lucian found this house. He met Tristan, the man who lives here. Tristan offered to trade medicines for goods and training. But when your father told Elias, he made him promise not to tell about the house. Elias caused a fire that killed Tristan's wife and... nearly killed him, too."

Draven's head is slightly cocked, his eyes unblinking.

"Tristan's wife, Victoria, didn't want to die. So she remained here, in this house, with him as her prisoner. She fed off of his life force to try to stave off her own decay."

His nostrils are flaring. "Victoria?"

I nod. "You met her."

His dark eyes narrow slightly. I know he's thinking that she had body enough to torment him.

"She isn't supposed to be here. She should be in the Netherworld. All of her feeding has created the darkness. A rift between our world and the next. I'm doing everything I can to stop it but –"

"But the shadows in the forest – the darkness started before my father's death."

"Your father wanted to break his vow of secrecy. He wanted to seek help from cities beyond our borders. Where Tristan and Victoria came from. Telling others about Tristan would draw attention to what Elias had done to them. So Elias killed Lucian and made it look like an accident."

The goblet of water in Draven's hand is shaking. Some is sloshing over so I gently take it from him.

"That's why he killed Scarlet," I say quietly. "She found out about what he did. She wasn't a witch."

Draven is stiff, his eyes focused on something just beyond my shoulder. His jaw clenched. This is enough to take in for now. He digs his fingers into his ponytail, making it messier than it already is. He shakes his head then closes his eyes as it aggravates his wound.

"Elias is no fool. What made him so threatened?"

This question has been in the back of my mind, as well. And I think I have an answer. "Us."

The focus in Draven's eyes shifts. He's looking at my face now.

"The more we know of the world, the more we may want to change. Learn to read. Try new medicines. Ideas. Until one day, we'd wake up and realize he knows nothing."

Draven's biting the inside of his lower lip.

"You've been gone a long while," he says. "After what happened to you and Scarlet, many of us lost faith in him. He has forbidden us from trying to flee. He has instituted a curfew. We're not allowed out of our homes. Sneaking out like I did is illegal."

Draven's bandage is blossoming with red. He shouldn't be talking.

"There are ten of us. A group I've armed. If I didn't come back with a kill, we were going to stop the lottery."

Revolt. Elias' worst fear is coming true under his nose and he is unaware. That gives me satisfaction. Now that we're warm and away from Victoria, I can hear myself.

I loathe Elias. I want him dead. Draven must, as well.

He's watching me with his head slightly cocked and the firelight is pooling in his eyes. The expression on his face has me worried his ribs aren't just cracked or broken. I'm worried they're stabbing something inside.

"I've missed you," he whispers. He *is* being stabbed inside, but not by his ribs. And now he's trying to stab me as well.

I take a deep breath and let it out. How do I explain to him what has happened? In fact, how do I explain it at all? I adore a man who is only half alive. A man who doesn't even have a body right now. A man who is kind and selfless and gentle. A man who killed his wife. A man who is in part causing the darkness, even if it isn't his doing. A man who should be the enemy.

"I wondered," he continues quietly. "If I would see you again after I died."

The roots he has grown in my chest are digging into me and it hurts. He would've looked for me in the Netherworld. And I would've looked for him. Because no matter how I feel about Tristan, Draven is my oldest friend.

Others in the village often mock him behind his back for muteness. He isn't quiet because he doesn't think. He sees more than anyone I've ever known. If I'm a Listener, then he's a watcher. He can read the slightest twitch or shift of weight and interpret a person's thoughts. Like he did when he realized how I had changed while I was with Tristan.

Draven's expression turns stony. I've missed my chance to say something. He knows we can never go back to how we were. He doesn't need words to see it in my face. He winces as he shoves himself up from the chair.

"Where are you going?" I ask.

He can't bend over so he crouches beside his crossbow a few feet away, abandoned when Victoria attacked him. He straightens and looks it over.

"The lottery begins when the moon sets." He hitches his crossbow to his belt. "I should travel while there's still some light."

Draven heads for the door and I grab his arm.

"You need to rest."

"If I rest, someone may die." He yanks his arm away and steps into the entryway.

"You'll lose too much blood. You'd freeze to death and no one would ever know."

He yanks open the door and descends the stairs. Snow is fluttering about in the moonlight.

"Draven!"

He pivots to face me. "Don't worry, Willow," he says mockingly. "After I'm dead, you'll still be able to hear my whispers. It'll make no difference. Because you've always ignored what I've been shouting."

Draven's roots are constricting inside, choking me. I wish I could speak. I wish I could say something to end this moment. To reverse it. But I can't. He gives me one last look, as if saying that he knows it's safe to leave me. That I can fend off Victoria without his help. Then he holds a hand to his bruised chest and turns away. He disappears into the forest, and all I can do is stand here on the porch and watch him go. Because his roots are so twisted up inside of me that I can't detangle them enough to think.

I'm getting cold so I slip back inside. Now that I truly am alone, the solitude of the house hits me. My skin crawls and I feel vulnerable. I gather firewood from the kitchen. The once plentiful stack has dwindled. I take a risk and climb the stairs. Once back inside our room, I lock the door then stir the ashes and start a fire.

Draven's right. I don't need him to protect me. I can protect myself. And having him here only makes things worse. Victoria lured him to the house to try to break me. If not for Scarlet, she would have succeeded.

The fire is roaring. Too hot for me to sit on the hearth. I grab Tristan's journal. Where is he? Doesn't he know I need him? What if he can't reform his body? How long should I wait? I think of Grandma Abella talking to someone who wasn't there. What if it was just someone no one could see? Someone like Tristan. And the only way to be with him was to kill herself.

The thought sends a chill down my back. I focus on the journal I'm holding. His handwriting is elegant loops on the page. Loops that mean nothing to me. I throw it across the room. My life is broken and it isn't fair. It isn't from poor choices I made or wicked things I've done. It's out of my control. I want to take control.

Looking at the fire, I wonder what will happen if I set the house ablaze. Victoria will have no halls to haunt. No doors to slam. No lamps to flicker. Fire, the creator and destroyer of Victoria's existence. It ended her once. Maybe it can again.

I grab a burning branch and carefully remove it from the flames. I look around the room. The books. They will burn well. I grab one and open it, laying it on the desk, exposing its pages. So many printed shapes lining the paper. I lower the flame. It's about to catch when the fire I'm holding snuffs out.

Smoke curls around my face. Irritation blooms in my chest. Then the fire dims. Someone shuffles in the darkness. The fire begins to recover as the heat claims more wood. The room slowly brightens.

Tristan is huddled in the corner, his head tucked into his arms, like a frightened child. Relief floods me as I toss the branch back into the flames and cross over to him. I sit down with my back against the wall, our shoulders touching. I wait for him to react but he doesn't. Not for a while.

"Why," he whispers, "did he bring about that horrible day? Why couldn't he just leave us alone?"

"I don't know." He did hear what I told Draven. I twine my arm with his, comforted by his warmth. He feels whole. I want to lie down in his wholeness.

"My back was to the fire when it caught," he says quietly. "Victoria was sitting on the hearth. She had asked me to bring her a blanket. I was walking away when I felt the pressure in the room change. Then heat and fire were everywhere, all over me. My back was burning so I dropped and rolled. I could smell melting hair. I could see the flames eating Victoria. I used the blanket to beat them out but my sleeves caught on fire, as well. We were both screaming."

He lifts his head. His bangs are in his face as he rests his chin on his hands.

"When it was finally out, I thought she was dead. I couldn't even recognize her. She lay there moaning while I put out the rest of the fire that had already eaten through the walls around the chimney."

"You did the best you could."

He rests his cheek on his hands as he peers at me. It's been too long since I've seen his face. I've forgotten how warm it makes me feel. "Will Draven be all right?"

I look away. Guilt gnaws at my stomach but it was his choice to leave. "He is a woodsman, like his father."

"Who died because of me. So much death because of me." His eyes have that terrible sadness again. "I deserve this prison. This torture. I let her take from me because I owe her life. I owe her life because I gave her death."

I touch my fingers to the curve of his cheekbone and turn his head to look at me. My voice is firm. "Her death was not your fault. You killed her to end her suffering. If anyone's to blame, it's Elias."

He shakes his head. "This is what you don't understand. What you've never understood. I wanted her to die. Long before she was burnt. I wanted to be free of her."

Clarity invigorates me like a breath of cold air. It is not his love for Victoria that has bound him to her after her death. It was not his loyalty to his dead wife that stopped him from lying with me. It was guilt. Not just over the mercy killing of his wife, but over having wished her dead. Gone. And then receiving what he wished for.

Watching Victoria languish in such agony was the most horrible thing I have ever experienced next to my sister's death. No one should suffer like that. Not even someone as manipulative as Victoria. She may have abused Tristan's trust and affection, but she didn't deserve to linger in such pain. And watching her suffer when there was nothing he could do to help her, feeling as if his dark thoughts had brought this upon her, changed Tristan even more than her death. He'll never be free of her until he lets go of his own remorse.

"You didn't bring death upon her."

He shakes his head. "If I never met Lucian. If we never came here –"

"If you never met her in the first place. If you were never born," I continue for him. "If, if, if. You can't change what has happened. The important thing is that you never intended for harm to come to her. If you really wanted her dead, you would've killed her yourself."

Tristan raises his brows, his eyes earnest, as if he doesn't think I understand. "But *if* I had never set those events in motion –"

"Then I never would've met you."

The concern on his face shifts. As if he feels small. Humbled. My fingers trace the side of his face.

"And despite all of the terrible things that have happened because of the darkness, I am so grateful to have met you. To feel the way I do. You make me happy and I want to return that happiness to you."

His lips twitch in a bashful smile. "You have." He cups my face. "Oh, you have."

Tristan presses his lips against mine. So warm and soft. Strong and gentle. And for several moments, I am lost in the rush of my own blood, the tickling of his hair against my fingers. The beauty he is radiating through me.

When he pulls away, he has a funny look on his face. As if he's been drinking. I know my expression matches his. And I'm so overwhelmed by the adorableness before me that I kiss him again.

"This is what it's meant to be," he murmurs against my lips before pulling away a little. "This happy quietness. This warmth. This delight."

I have nothing else to compare to how we feel. No, I do. I have his memories. The sordid passion of Victoria. The mixing of pain and pleasure. The withdrawals and indulgences. All he knew of love until now. I kiss him again to let him know he is right.

This trust and contentment. This giving and receiving. This is love.

We linger with our faces close together, our skin touching. His breath falls on my chin and neck. He smells of autumn leaves and sweat. His hand is in mine, his thumb stroking my skin, drawing teasing shapes. Everything else fades away but this moment. These sensations. This togetherness.

At length, the pleasant tickling stops. He shifts. "I know what I have to do," he whispers. I nod.

Squeezing my hand, he rises and I rise with him. We start for the door. He unlocks it and I press myself closer to his side as we enter the hall. The only light in the house is coming from the fireplace downstairs. No moonlight lingers on the sills. It must be day. I wonder if Draven made it back to Morrot. If they stopped the lottery.

We walk down the hall, towards the chained door. My hair stands on end as we near. I know she's in there. But she is still weak. Tristan pulls a key out of his breast pocket and slides it into the lock that binds the chains together. I watch his hand, waiting for him to turn it. Tensing. Instead, he looks at me with worry tinting his eyes.

"If this works," he says, "Then I'll be like you. I won't be able to heal myself with fire anymore."

I nod but the concern hasn't left his face.

"I'll have my scars."

And then it hits me. He's not worried about injuries. He's worried that I won't want him anymore. That I'll be disgusted by his burns. I called him a monster once. I catch his hand in mine and kiss it.

"Your body is beautiful to me because it's yours. Nothing can change that."

Tristan's expression softens. He looks like he's about to cry. Instead, he lets go of the lock and grabs me in a hug. I cling to him as he buries his nose in my hair. I kiss his neck. We hold each other until his heartbeat calms. Then he pulls away and turns the key.

The lock clicks and he removes it from the chains. Then he tugs and the metal links slither as he coils them until the door is bare. He sets them aside. I take his hand again as he sticks the key in the final lock and turns. The bolt thuds. He tries the handle and the door slowly creaks open.

Chapter Twenty-Two

The room before us is dark and smells of the forest. Several lamps burst to life within as Tristan wills light into the room. It's their bedroom. The wall around the chimney is missing, bordered by charred planks of wood. It is letting in a chill and something else.

Snow. It's lightly dusting everything in the room. Even the old cobwebs. In the darkness of the sky, the snowflakes look like they're appearing right above our heads.

The floor creaks as we step forward. I see the bed, still stained dark with old blood and burnt flesh. The nightstand beside it looks as it did in Tristan's memory. The knife rests upon it next to an empty glass. Along the other wall is a chest of drawers. A vase is set on lace. Dried roses clustered. Above the chest of drawers is a large painting. I pause when I see it.

Though it has been dulled by exposure to the elements, it is shockingly lifelike. Tristan and Victoria pose by an armchair. She seated in it, him beside with his hand resting on her shoulder. A corner of the frame and canvas are charred, peeling and bubbling from the heat of the fire.

"Victoria painted that," Tristan says quietly.

"She was a wonderful artist," I say.

And I mean it. In all this madness I have forgotten that she was a woman. She was once more than her faults. Tristan lets go of my hand as he crosses over to the fireplace. The river rock is blackened and cracked. Even now, the scent of old smoke lingers. A half-burned blanket is on the ground where Tristan left it all those years ago. He sucks in a shaky breath as he gazes at the hearth.

I cross to him and hug his arm. He turns away and closes his eyes. Though it didn't happen to me, I felt what it was like for Tristan. And I don't like being here anymore than he does. But when we pivot to face the bed and I gaze upon the dark stains, I am reminded of more than Victoria. I hear the echo of Scarlet's screams as she died. Two women who never knew each other in life. Such opposites. Both burned. And by the same hand.

Tristan takes one of the dried roses out of the vase. He tugs on the blossom until it pops off into his hand. I let go of him as he steps forward and scatters the petals on the bed. I remember him saying he used to sleep like that when he was kept from Victoria. The passion wasn't all one-sided.

Then he sits on the side of the mattress, as if she were lying there. He runs his hand across the snowy, charred fabric. Then he lies down. I feel out of place. But he wanted me here. He rests his hand where her hips would have been.

"I'm so sorry, Victoria," he whispers. His voice is strained and I realize he is crying. "I'm so sorry that this happened to you. So sorry that I couldn't help you. That I couldn't make the world stable for you." He sniffs and a tear slips down his cheek.

My breath hitches in my throat as the bed beside him dents. Like someone is lying there. I quietly step to the side. There, between the lamplight and snow, I can glimpse the shimmering image of Victoria. She is gazing at Tristan with empathy and affection. An expression I've never seen her wear. And though I can see her, my hair isn't standing on end.

"For a few moments, you did," she says. Her voice is ethereal and though I could clearly make out the words, I wonder if I heard it at all.

"Our moments are over," he whispers. His hand is now holding her ghost hand. "It's time to say goodbye."

"Will you ever forgive me?" she asks.

Tristan kisses her shimmering knuckles. "I already do."

"I'm frightened without you." Her eyes are glistening. "What is beyond the Netherworld?"

My mind tightens and it's as if I'm no longer standing on the floor as realization strikes. My gift is suddenly illuminated. The only dead I can hear are the restless, because only the restless linger in the Netherworld. The rest pass on. To where or what, I don't know. And neither does Victoria.

That's why I've only ever heard my sister when she wanted to help me end the darkness. To bring her killer to justice. To save our family. But unlike Victoria, Scarlet is not afraid. If she was, she wouldn't have used all of her strength helping me last night. She would've used it to ask for my help instead, like all the others. Like Victoria fighting to remain in her body. Not because she loved Tristan, but because she was afraid of what lies beyond.

"Don't be afraid," I whisper.

I don't know what lies beyond, but I know from Scarlet that it isn't any more frightening than anything unknown. Like kissing a boy without knowing if he'll kiss you back, we either have nothing to lose or everything to gain.

I can sense Victoria. I welcome her fear into my body and fill her with my assurance of hope. "Don't be afraid."

Victoria closes her eyes and her shimmering body drifts apart, piece by piece, into snowflakes. A gust of wind cuts through the hole in the wall and she scatters, shimmering flecks spinning about in the room. I hear a whisper of thanks in my mind. Then the snowflakes fade into the darkness of the sky.

As Tristan lets out a shaky breath, I wrap my mind around what I've just done. I brought her peace. Like so many other restless spirits. It just took much more to get her to accept her fate. To let go of the living. To build the courage to move on. And now I know why I came to this house. Why I was right all along. It had to be me.

Tristan sits up. As he looks to me, the wound on his cheek appears, the wound Victoria gave him as she clawed at his face in agony before he killed her. It streams blood for a moment then slowly closes itself up. He rolls up his sleeves to examine his arms. The burns are ugly but so long as they don't pain him, I don't care. His half-living over these five years has allowed his body some healing.

He looks away from me. I cross over and kneel beside him. Once again, I tear off part of my dress and clean the blood off his face. And I smile because now I know he is real.

Pale scars from her fingernails run down the side of his face from his temple to his cheek. His skin is no longer perfectly smooth, his beauty no longer vulnerable. Fine lines rim his eyes. Though he's clean-shaven, the shadow of stubble is on his jaw. Cares and hopes and pain have etched his gaze with age. Experience. He is a man. Yet as he timidly returns my smile, I realize that I was right. Nothing could take away the innocence of his beauty.

I throw my arms around him in a hug then kiss him. Tristan holds me, shaking slightly, and I know all of the sensations of being fully human again are bombarding him.

"Come," I say, tugging on his hand. There is something I need to do.

He rises and follows me as I gently pluck a rose from the vase. We leave the room behind. As we head down the hall, I feel as if a weight has lifted from the house. I descend the stairs without worry. I light a candle and take it with us. Remembering the snow, I put my slippers back on. Once outside, we pick our way to the back of the house. I shove aside the metal gate and we cross over to Victoria's grave. I rest the rose beside her tombstone then hug Tristan's arm. His scars are smooth and lumpy under my fingers. I kiss them.

The rose on the grave slowly brightens in color. At first I think it's a trick of the candle's flame, then Tristan tenses. He sees it, too. The rose is slowly blossoming, coming back to life. Its red and green are beautiful. Made all the more beautiful when I realize that I'm not only viewing it from the light of the candle. I can see the snow falling around me. I can see Tristan's face. I can see the faintest outline of the clouds. The darkness is lifting.

Tristan grins. I wrap my arms around his neck. Laughing and crying at the same time. He spins me about, lifting my feet off the ground. I feel like I'm flying. He sets me down and kisses me. I would kiss him back longer but I'm still laughing.

Pulling away, I hold out my arms. I watch as snowflakes drift about. They're gathering in our hair, on our lashes. The snow on the ground seems unnaturally bright as the world lightens. It's like getting my vision back after being blind. I can't get enough of gazing at everything. I can't get enough of Tristan's face, and he can't get enough of mine. He tucks one of my stray curls behind my ear.

Then I hear something in the distance. A man screaming for help.

Chapter Twenty-Three

Tristan has heard it, as well. His smile fades. We both look to the woods. The growing light is like dusk. It's difficult to make out shapes. I step away from Tristan and towards the sound. The new snow makes the forest appear clean.

"Help!" I hear again.

My eyes dart to movement in the distance. A brown shape is making its way through the snow, stumbling.

"It's a man," Tristan says, stepping to my side. "Look."

He points out something I didn't see. They're hard to glimpse through the shadowy air and falling snow, but lights dance through the trunks deeper in. Lanterns. A hunt. The lottery. They're going to kill someone. Draven was already weak, an easy victim.

Gathering up my skirt, I run towards the man.

"Willow!" Tristan follows me. "You'll catch your death."

"It might be Draven," I shout over my shoulder. "Or my mother. My father."

Tristan jogs to catch up. He keeps pace with me for several yards until I slow. The man fleeing from the mob appears encumbered. My breath fogs before me and I have to keep blinking in the brightness of the snow. It will take a while to adjust to this light. For all of us. But I welcome the challenge.

"There." Tristan touches my arm as he points out the figure.

The man is running towards us. I am about to jog out to meet him when I realize why he's encumbered. Robes. Brown robes. Elias.

This changes everything. If Elias is fleeing a mob then Draven was successful. The lottery ignited rebellion. Morrot has turned on its leader. Tristan lets go of my arm and starts to dart towards the man but I stop him.

"Don't. It's Elias. He's the Bringer."

Tristan's eyes widen as he snaps his head back to look at the face of the man who caused so much pain.

Elias is nearing us. His cheeks are flushed, his pale eyes wild. "Help!" he screams again.

The lanterns are nearer. I can make out the shapes of their bearers. A figure is racing ahead of them. Impossibly fast and graceful upon the fresh snow. Long legs. Draven.

"Good people," Elias sputters as he nears.

I look over my shoulder. We're close enough that he can see the house. He must think that he failed. That Tristan and I are the couple he tried to kill. That we'll seek to help a stranger in need.

"Please. Help me!"

Tristan darts from my side. He runs towards Elias. I'm close enough to see Elias' face break into a smile of relief as Tristan approaches. I gather up my dress and follow.

"Thank you, good sir! Thank you!" He holds out his hands, tripping as he runs.

Tristan is near him but doesn't slow. Elias' smile starts to fade as he notices. But he doesn't notice fast enough to avoid Tristan's fist ramming into his temple. He collapses with a sputter, sinking into the snow, cupping his bleeding ear.

"She suffered for days!" Tristan roars. He kicks Elias in the head, knocking the elder man onto his back. "You heartless bastard!"

Tristan is about to kick him again but Elias is so frail he can't take much more.

I grab Tristan's arm. "You're not a killer!"

Tristan yanks away from me and readies to kick Elias again. The older man cowers, whimpering as blood pours from his nose. I can hear the shouts of the villagers. Tristan restrains himself and meets my gaze. His eyes have a fire in them I've never seen, the fire of flowing blood and taut muscles.

"You're not a killer," I repeat.

He looks back to Elias with a sneer. "You're right," he says, taking a step back towards me. "I'm not."

I know Elias killed my sister. He's the reason she's not here and so much more. But looking at him now, I only see a frightened old man. A weak excuse for a human being.

Someone in the mob is shouting at us to stop him. They're near enough that I can just make out their faces. My heart leaps when I realize that my family may be among them. I can't wait to feel their arms, to share them with Tristan. Draven is nearing us, crossbow in hand.

I look back to Elias. He is shaking, staring at me with frightened eyes. Like an animal in a snare. Then recognition flashes. He knows who I am. I can't look at him anymore. The old man is fading. I'm seeing my sister's killer. And I don't trust myself to have the restraint that Tristan has shown. Neither does he, apparently. Tristan is tugging on my hand, leading me back to the house. I spit on Elias then follow. Let the villagers deal with him.

Hugging Tristan's arm to my side, I march towards the house. We're several steps away when I hear the scream. A maddened, desperate sound. I look over my shoulder and see Elias on his feet, his weakness faded. Sprinting at us with a raised knife.

I am about to shove Tristan out of the way when a bolt sticks in Elias' wrist. He drops the knife and lets out a howl. Gripping his wounded arm, he falls to his knees.

I spot Draven in the distance. His bandage is blood-stained, his hair wild. But his body is cool and calm as he lowers his crossbow. Falcon eyes indeed.

He casts the weapon aside then pulls out his hunting knife and stalks towards Elias like prey. I realize what he's about to do but I don't try to stop him. Tristan may not be a killer, but Draven is.

Elias is whimpering, writhing about as he clutches his wrist. His sounds grow more panicked as Draven nears. I squeeze Tristan's arm and he grabs my hand, hugging it to his warm chest.

"No, no please," Elias is pleading. "Please, boy."

Draven's boots crunch in the snow as he straddles the wounded man. Readying the knife, he yanks it across Elias' throat without even blinking. Elias's pleading becomes gurgled wheezing. He thumps as his body sinks into the snow. Then Draven cleans his knife and straightens, as calm as if he'd just killed a deer and not a man. And so the Bringer of Darkness leaves this world. No pomp and circumstance. Just metal and blood.

The mob is nearing. Their lanterns are dull in the growing brightness. They slow as they notice their quarry is no longer stirring. As they notice the house. Draven pivots and sheathes his knife in his belt. He stands before his kill, facing the villagers.

Tristan cups my face and turns it towards his. He doesn't want me staring at the body. He rests his forehead against mine and I smile. I lay my hand over his on my cheek. I can hear the crunching snow of the approaching villagers. Friends and family.

The clouds part and the sun illuminates the forest. It is so bright against the snow that I nearly have to shut my eyes. Then Tristan jerks and a puff of breath hits my lips. I open my eyes. He hasn't moved but something is wrong. It's too bright. All around us is glowing whiteness. All I can see are his eyes. They're colored with surprise but the surprise fades. All that remains is affection. Then his hand falls away from my face and I scream. I scream because I know what's happened before I see it.

Catching his waist, I fall to my knees with him as his legs give out. His blood is spattering my mother's wedding dress. A crossbow bolt is sticking out of his heart. I scream again. A woman in the crowd gasps and shrieks, as well. Hurried footsteps dash towards her. I hear Draven yelling.

The sun is no longer too bright as I look upon Tristan's pleasant face once more. He isn't pained. He's reposed. I cup his cheek.

"Tristan..."

Tears are pooling in my eyes and I try to blink them away. I won't let them mar my last view of my beloved.

One of his hands is still holding mine. He squeezes it.

"I love you," he whispers.

Heat is racing through me. This is happening too fast. I can't understand it. He can't be leaving. He can't. I just brought him back. Tristan clenches his jaw as a spasm courses through his torso. He is in pain. Again. We cannot be created for such suffering.

I lean forward until all I can see is him. I comb my fingers through his soft hair. I press my lips to his. Though they're already cooling, he's all I know. He's all I feel. And the rest of the world fades away again, leaving us alone for one last time, wrapped in each other. And I remember how he fills me with warmth. With life. How we danced in the moonlight. *One, two, three.*

"I'll always love you," I whisper against his lips.

Tristan squeezes my hand. I lift my head just high enough to see his eyes. The pale light around us is shining in them, filling them with wonder. Innocence. Love. And for a few more precious heartbeats, it's just us. Just us and our light in the darkness.

Then his hand grows limp. I squeeze it but he doesn't squeeze back. The wonder in his eyes fades. His chest doesn't stir against mine. An empty body. He has been ripped from me, taking my heart and any sense left in the world with him.

My lungs have stopped working. All I can hear are horrible choking sounds. Like someone being fed upon. Then I realize they're coming from me. I lay my head on Tristan's chest, listening for a heartbeat I know I won't find. But why can't I find it? It was here just moments ago. Just moments. I won't let go of his hand. I shake as I sob against his chest. His still chest. I'm leaking from my eyes and nose but I don't care. He's growing cold beneath me. No. I won't let him.

Don't grow cold, Tristan. Don't leave me.

After a while I realize that someone is touching my head. They have been for some time now. They try to pry me away from Tristan but I fight. I scream. I keen. Through my tears, I think I glimpse my father but I don't care. This is my place. This is where I belong. By his side evermore. Even if he has grown cold. Even if he has left me.

An arm slips around my waist and hoists me up. I'm too weak to fight. Someone is trying to keep me on my feet. It's my father again. Below me is Tristan's body, still and peaceful. The white snow around him stained red with his blood. So red. He needs me.

I try to lunge for him again, to curl up at his side and wait for my own death, but my father stops me. He speaks to me but I can't understand the words. I can't understand anything. He's trying to lead me away. He is strong and I have no choice but to drag my feet behind him. As I start to move, I see Draven's mother. She is weeping. She wails something at me but I might as well not have ears.

Then I see Draven standing there, watching me. Looking at me as if I were Lady. Those dark eyes pooled with tears, his breath clouding before his face.

Everything is so bright. So nonsensical. Where am I going?

Tristan. I have to get to Tristan. I try to twist away to dash back to my beloved. But I am suddenly floating. Father is carrying me. I can see the sky and it's blinding me. Blinding. I close my eyes.

Chapter Twenty-Four

I lie in bed and listen to the world around me. My back is turned to our hearth. I am facing the wall, as I have for days. Voices echo to me from the center of the village. Axes chop, digging into wood. I hear Megan laugh some distance away, laughing because she is sunburned. I close my eyes. I try to shut out the sounds of life around me. I don't want them. For what is life without Tristan?

My mother sets a bowl of stew down beside me. I can hear the rustle of her dress. Smell the herbs of the broth. I don't want it. I won't eat. I haven't since he died days ago. And I don't intend to. My mother lingers for a moment, hoping I'll stir. I hold extra still. Pretend I'm asleep. She leaves.

Maybe I do sleep. When I wake, my parents and Jasper are trying to speak in hushed voices. They're trying not to disturb me. I ignore their conversations. I don't want to hear how Draven has been asking for me. How it was his mother who picked up his fallen crossbow. How it was his mother who thought she was killing the fiend who had nearly killed her son. The sunlight was so bright. All she had seen were Tristan's horrible scars. All she saw was monster, not man. So she fired.

Instead, I focus on how Tristan lay behind me in bed, filling me with such warmth and protection. How he sang as we danced. Laughed as I twirled.

"*For without you I'm a flower gone dry,*

A ship without sails,

A star without a sky." I whisper to the night.

No one in the house stirs. It's dark. Time has slipped past me again. And I don't like it because I get confused. My memories of Tristan are becoming jumbled. I can't order them properly. I can't find the ones that feel the most real. Everything is slipping away with me.

The next morning, I awake to a sound I haven't heard in ages. A songbird. Its ululating melody is so charming that I wish Tristan was here to listen. At least he got to see the sunlight again, though that's little comfort since he's not here to enjoy it. Hot tears are on my cheeks. This is like Scarlet's death all over again. As soon as I regain my strength, I cry.

A bowl of porridge is left on the quilt beside me. I didn't even hear my mother approach. I sniffle and cover my face, trying to hide. My hair itches as I move. It has matted into rugs that tug at my scalp. I smell. But I like my wretchedness.

"Lil?" comes a soft voice.

I hold still and listen. That's not my mother's voice. It's Jasper's. He rests his small hand on my shoulder.

"I don't want you to die, too," he whispers.

I roll over to look at him. My vision is blurry in the overcast light. I blink to clear it. Jasper's grey eyes are timid, his thin face drawn. But his color is coming back. He may yet grow tall.

Sniffling, I hold my hand out for his. He takes it and climbs into bed with me. He rests his head in the crook of my neck.

"Everyone dies," I whisper. I'm surprised by the hoarseness of my own voice. My mouth is dry.

"I know that," Jasper says. "That doesn't mean we can't live."

Live. Can I still be counted among the living? Am I living? I am. Barely. I'm forgetting. Everything. Like a spirit. Because I'm letting myself die.

Jasper shifts and grabs the bowl of porridge. He holds it in front of me. I see the worry in his eyes. He no longer has the faith that his big sister will do what's right. So I do what I haven't done in days. I prop myself up and take a bite. Jasper smiles.

Maybe it was the birdsong. Maybe it was Jasper feeding me instead of my mother. But I'm thinking more clearly. I've bitten my fingernails down to stubs. I've stopped trying to sort through my memories of Tristan, because all of them are important. And I've tried to relive them so much that they're becoming dull. Faded. I don't want him to fade. Ever.

That night, I hear my parents talking. This time I listen. My mother mentions that Draven has asked for me again. My father sighs. The next day, while my family is out, I get up. I wash my body and comb my hair. I put on a clean dress. I slip my feet into boots. By the time I make it to the door, I'm dizzy. I need to eat more.

I stagger outside, squinting in the sunlight. The sky is still overcast but I feel the pale light on my skin like heat from a lamp. I don't want to be seen. I don't want to answer any questions. So instead of walking through the village, I circle around it. Slow, steady steps. I close my eyes and tilt my head to the sky, soaking in the light. I hold my hands out like a bird gliding. Like Lady soaring.

I'm not better. There is no better. But I need to feel the sun. For Scarlet. For Tristan. I start twining pieces of dead grass into a bracelet. My wandering has brought me to Draven's barn. The hens used to live here. Draven used to sneak outside to sleep with Lady here. Draven.

His mother steps outside, carrying a bucket to the well. I look at the ground instead of her face. Her hands which released the bolt. Released my sanity. While she is out, I shuffle into his house.

The place is quiet. Only ashes glow in the hearth. Draven is in bed. Isn't it late? I thought I was the only one who stayed in bed at all hours. I let my fingertips drag across the wall, feeling the rough logs as I step over to him. His eyes open at the scuff of my boots. His face and neck are slicked with moisture. Fever.

I sink down into the chair beside his bed.

"They didn't tell me you were sick," I say.

The flush of his cheeks and the scent of his sweat invigorate me. He smells like death. The hole in his neck hasn't healed. Angry red skin surrounds it. His eyes are tired and glossy but they find mine. I hold his dark gaze. Several moments pass. Then he shivers and I pull the pelts up over his bare shoulders. He shifts to lie on his side.

Birds sing outside. I wonder if he hears them. I hope he knows I'm here. He hunches his back as if he has feathers to ruffle. I tuck the pelts under his chin. One of his wrists is uncovered, resting against the straw mattress. The skin there is crisscrossed with white scars from Lady. I remember when the falcon first hatched. Draven spoke more back then. I made a bracelet that day. I have one in my hands.

Draven watches me with half-lidded eyes as I slip the dry grass bracelet onto his wrist. He studies it for some time, never moving more than the rise and fall of his chest. Eventually, his eyes drift shut and he sleeps. I kiss his damp brow then leave. By the time I get home, I only have the strength to crawl into bed and sleep. For the first time since I can remember, I dream. Of butterflies. Such colors. When I wake, I remember Tristan.

He had dreamed of butterflies, as well. Had thought that they must be jealous of him. Because while they had bodies longer than he did, he had his long enough to feel the sun. And my hand. And that was enough for him. I look at my hand. Pale and lined. I open and close it. There is nothing special about it. It was only special when our palms touched. I close my eyes and sigh but I do not weep. Not tonight.

I wake up from pounding on the door. The light is gray. Before dawn. Jasper stirs first, pulling a blanket around him in my parents' bed as my father rises. He answers the door and Draven's mother dashes in. I stiffen at the sight of her. She is sobbing. I want to throw something at her. Scream for her to get out.

"I'm so sorry," she wails against my father's chest. He reluctantly pats her back then looks over his shoulder at my mother. She hurries out of bed and hugs her friend.

"What is it Gwen? Is it Draven?"

Gwen nods, her face flushed and shining. Tears. I don't care if she's wretched. I still want to hit her. I'm standing. I didn't even notice getting up.

"He won't wake up. I'm being punished. This is my punishment," Gwen moans.

My mother gazes at me as she rubs Gwen's back. Then Gwen notices me. She stumbles towards me, her hair a rat's nest, her bony hands reaching for mine.

"I'm so sorry, Willow. So sorry for what I've done."

She grabs my hand and falls to her knees. She presses her wet cheek against my skin. She is sobbing. I yank my hand away and dart out of the room, out into the grey light.

My nightgown is thin and the air is crisp but there is no snow. I run on bare feet. I run into the forest. I want to keep going to the house. To see if Tristan is there without a body. To lie where he lay. But instead, I stop in a clearing. What used to be a meadow. Green shoots are sprouting all over, surprisingly tall. The naked trees are adorned with buds.

Spring is coming. Draven is dying. Tristan is dead. I fall to my knees.

I want to weep. I try to force myself to weep. Nothing comes out. So I throw a rock. It bounces off a trunk and disappears in the dead leaves. So much death. So much suffering. Is this the reason for life? An endless string of goodbyes? I want to say goodbye to Draven but I can't bring myself to move. I'm weak. I can't watch another death. Another body fail.

Warmth kisses my hands. My arms. My chest. I look up. The sun is peeking over the ridge, rising in the east. The clouds are scattered. For the first time in years, I feel its golden light. I close my eyes as it bathes my face.

"Hello."

I open my eyes. The heat is making the damp trees and ground steam. I glimpse movement in the moisture. The mist before me thickens. There, between the crystalline water and sunlight, is a shimmering image. I blink several times to make sure I'm seeing it. I am.

Tristan's face grows clearer as the sun rises. I suck in a shaky breath. He smiles

Whispers swirl in my mind. They're his and I've missed them. I reach for him and tickles gather in my hand as he takes it in his. I climb to my feet.

He touches my face. I don't feel his fingers, just his warmth. It leaves me glowing and I smile. He smiles, too, and the sight is so welcomed that I am filled with such delight that I don't know what to do with myself. The tears have finally returned. He rests his forehead against mine. Affection and pressure on my skin.

"I miss you so much," I whisper.

"I would have stayed with you."

My tears are drying quickly in this sunlight. The longing in his eyes cuts into me, reflecting my own. Then it fades and he smiles. "You're simple again."

He shakes his head. "Not simple. Pure. How we all are inside."

Pure. No distractions from our complicated minds. No motives or intentions. Just being. Blissful being.

"You freed me, Willow."

He tugs my hand out above me with an impish expression. I smile as I twirl away from him then back. One last dance. He is grinning. My skin is tickling with delight.

Then his smile dims. His eyes bore into mine. "I need you to do something for me," he says.

"Anything."

"I need you to not be afraid."

I feel my own smile disappearing. I'm not a spirit. I'm not leaving the Netherworld. I've already lost so much. What could I have to fear?

More loss. More pain. More goodbyes. That is what I fear. How can I not be afraid of losing the ones I love?

His eyes are clear as they gaze into mine. Does he know my thoughts?

"Don't be afraid," he says again. He eyes me for a moment, the smile returning. "Thank you." He leans in as if to kiss me, but he's fading. Disappearing with the shimmering mist. A light touch on my lips, tingling.

I want to see his face one last time, but it's already gone. Then I feel his warmth move through me. Blossom in my chest. Like a hug. A kiss. Then I have thoughts that aren't my own. Knowledge I never learned. One last gift.

I look at the forest around me. I need to find something. Tristan has shown me what. It's a plant with little almond-shaped leaves. Pungent. We used to hang it in the house to freshen up the air. It grew on the hillsides year-round. Thyme.

Running, I head for the nearest slope where I remember its purple flowers in the spring. Dead leaves and sticks. No plants. Shoving the debris around, I hunt for any sign of green. Because this plant will fight infection. Thyme will save Draven's life.

My hands and fingernails are filthy. I find shoots of grass. Dead roots. And I'm starting to panic because I can't find any sign of the plant. Which means Draven will die. He'll die and I'll say another goodbye. More hours and days of weeping.

No. I keep digging. I've done enough waiting. Enough moping. Tristan's request solidifies in my mind. My heart. It has nothing to do with saying goodbye and everything to do with saying hello.

Everyone fears loss. But when he asked me to not be afraid, it wasn't of losing someone. It was of loving someone. Loving someone in spite of knowing you will one day part. That takes courage. The courage that defined Scarlet. Courage I didn't know I possessed until I felt Tristan's warmth.

And then I find it. A sprig of baby leaves. Just a few. I rub them between my fingers and smell. It's thyme. But I need more of it. I yank up what I can then rummage through dead leaves like a boar. I don't stop until my arms and nightgown are caked with mud and debris. I now have a fistful of baby leaves full of oil.

I run back to the village, past our cabin. I'm sweating in the heat of the sun but I like it. I burst into Draven's house. His mother leaps up in surprise as I do so. Draven is pale and still. He looks dead. Am I too late?

No. His chest is rising and falling. His skin still slicked with a ghastly sheen. Gwen is asking me questions but I ignore her. I don't want to look at her. I follow the instructions Tristan left in my mind.

I wash off my hands. Grabbing a bowl and using a wooden spoon handle as a pestle, I mash the leaves up. I mash them for all I'm worth until they're bruised dark green and sticking together in clumps. Then I mash them some more. Well past when my arm and shoulder start burning from the labor. When it's oily enough, I carry it over to Draven's bed. I unwind his bandage.

The hole made from Victoria's teeth is clotted and mangled, the skin around it scarlet. I grab a cup of water from the bedside table and douse it, rinsing it out. Then I scrape the contents of the bowl into the wound. I use my finger to wipe out every last drop of oil. Gwen hands me a clean bandage and I bind the wound up once more. We will need more plants. More medicine if he is going to heal. But for now we will have to watch and wait.

His lips are pale and I can't look at his sickly face anymore. I cross over to the hearth as Gwen looks him over. My hands smell of thyme. I pace in front of the fire.

Don't be frightened.

There are strange baskets cluttered about with furs and carvings that aren't Draven's or Gwen's. Offerings, I realize. Meager gifts for the boy they all used to mock. The boy who freed them. Maybe they expect him to lead.

I get lost in my head. I don't know how much time passes, but sunlight is streaming in through the windows. Draven has yet to show any signs of life. My mother has somehow appeared and sits talking with Gwen in a corner.

I pinch my lip as I finally bring myself to look at her. Tristan's killer. All I see before me is a bereaved woman who feels like an aunt to me. A woman who is on the brink of losing everything. If Draven dies, she'll be alone. She made a mistake. A horrible mistake. Hunger drives people to the end of their wits. There was a mob. It was bright. She couldn't see properly. She thought she was protecting her child. My mother might have done the same. But more than that, I'm tired of seeing Gwen suffer. I stop pacing and I do what Tristan would want me to do. What he did a thousand times.

"Gwen?" I look at her out of the corner of my eyes as she turns her head towards me. "I forgive you," I mutter.

She stares at me. I start pacing again. I block her out once more as she starts to speak. No conversations right now. It was enough just to wrap my head around those three words.

They probably think I'm mad. Let them. I'm not. I'm light. I'm loved. I'm a sister. I'm Willow. And I will give.

Chapter Twenty-Five

The cool grass tickles my ears as I hold up my arm. My skin is deep golden. I run my hand against it. The rushing of the creek nearby is interrupted by a plop. I sit up to check on Jasper. I can see him over the stubby blackberry bushes. He's tossing rocks into the water as he wanders the bank. His dark hair is swept behind him in a ponytail. He is lean, but not from hunger. From growth. He will be tall like our father. Like Scarlet.

Draven has watched Jasper toss in a rock and mimics him. His dark eyes study the ripples he has caused. The scar on his neck stands out pale against the chestnut of his skin. We're both browner than we've ever been. And I like it that way. The green bracelet I braided for him this morning stands out all the more against his darkened flesh. He crouches as he picks up rocks as if he's suddenly discovered treasure on the ground. Jasper sees him hunching and wanders over. Draven holds a rock out to him then rises.

They each toss their rocks into the water, trying to skip them. When Jasper fails, he grabs another from Draven's hand. Jasper's second rock splashes the two and he giggles. Draven smiles then tries to make his rock splash, as well. They look like two little boys, only one is twice as tall.

Boys. My boys. Healthy and strong. Brown and alive.

I lay my head back down in the grass. The deep green of the leaves above give me peace. They whisper, their tips haloed in sunlight. I close my eyes. I feel a bite of sadness at their whispers. I miss Tristan.

But I am trying to make him proud. Trying to be happy for the both of us. Trying to maintain my courage. I am alive. Alive. A life.

Months have passed since Draven lay dying. Since I last felt Tristan's presence. But that's a good thing, I tell myself. It means he has moved on. He doesn't need my help anymore. The funny part is that I needed his. All along.

It took a dead man to remind me how to live.

I still miss him terribly. There have been many times when I've found myself wandering to his grave. No one really held a funeral. They would've buried him in our cemetery but the ground was too cold to dig. Instead they found a spot for him in the woods. I don't mind. He'd like it better there, anyway. Elias' body was conveniently forgotten.

I doubt I'll ever stop thinking about the day Tristan died. What I could have done differently. What could have saved him. But then I remind myself of the words I once spoke to him. *If, if, if.* A thousand ifs. A thousand possibilities, yet only one. Only one came true.

While I still weep at night for Scarlet and Tristan, I've learned that the only way I heal is by focusing on what I have, not what I've lost. So every night when I am about to sleep with Jasper at my side and crickets filling the air with song, I count my blessings. My family. My health. Food. How hard I laughed when Jasper fell asleep at cards then shot up when he woke, asking "Did I lose?" How happy Gwen's face is when she looks at her healthy son. The breadth of Draven's smile.

And oh, how he smiles. Enough for all of us. Like he's making up for all the smiles everyone missed during the darkness. He knows what a gift he's been given to live again. We all do now that the sun is back, but not like Draven. His delight in being out of bed, of movement without pain, is infectious. He's addicted to using his body.

Undaunted enthusiasm for experiencing novelty. Like a child. And that part of him reminds me of Tristan.

The light above me is blocked by a shadow. A hawk. He screeches as he circles our clearing, hunting for field mice, keeping an eye on his master. He is young and doesn't like to stray. He doesn't yet know how to hunt and bring back prey to Draven, but he'll learn. Draven doesn't seem like he's in a rush to train him. I think he really just enjoys the company. I do, as well. The hawk still has spotted feathers and the long legs of a youth, but he is beautiful. After asking my permission, Draven named him Tristan. In memory of the man who saved his life, and in honor of me.

A drop of cold water lands on my face and I hear Jasper squeal. Lots of splashing. Sitting up, I see that the two have gotten into a play fight. Jasper is running upstream, trying to get out of range to spray Draven back, but there is no out of range.

Two laughs, one high and one deep. I am smiling. Because when I hear Draven laugh and see his smile, I know that the roots he has grown in my chest never died. And now I wonder if they're growing something more. There are leaves and buds attached to the roots. Their presence is thrilling and humbling. Frightening. I'm doing my best not to be afraid. But still, I'm not ready for them to flower yet.

Draven slips on a rock and goes down. Jasper squeals in triumph and attacks. Enough watching.

I leap to my feet and dash over to join them. The water is cold and weighs down my dress but I let it get soaked. I join my brother in his onslaught and am rewarded by getting doused by Draven. I try to run away but I'm laughing too hard. He grabs my waist and yanks me down. I squeal as the cold is suddenly all over. But his chest is warm and my hand is resting upon the green bracelet on his wrist.

Our laughter rings out on the banks. In the green woods. The hillsides. The darkness is gone, but I will keep the lessons it taught me and the joy a young man brought me. For no matter what happens, what new flowers bloom in my chest, one will always belong to him. Evermore.

"Midsummer's Song"

Behold the joy of children
Behold the joy of men,
Behold the burning circle
That never has an end.

Through falling leaves and winter snow
The sun will visit those below
And warm the Netherworld will be
But it's not there that you'll find me.

Behold the joy of children
Behold the joy of men,
Behold the burning circle
That never has an end.

Through spring meadows and summer sky,
The sun will shine on you and I
For we are young and dance around
Bonfires shining above ground.

Behold the joy of children
Behold the joy of men,
Behold the burning circle
That never has an end.

Whether in this life or the next,
Even after sunset in the west
The light will return from high above
For it is my heart and you are my love.

Acknowledgments

Thank you to my wonderful family. This book would not have been possible without your support. To my sister, who is my other half and gives me such strength. To my brothers for years of laughter and roughhousing. To my parents who have always cherished and encouraged my imagination. To my friends for always accepting me for who I am. And to my grandparents for their love while alive, and for strolling the halls and hiding things when I'm not looking after death.

I love you all more than there are stars in the sky and waves in the sea.

And thank *you*, dear reader, for investing a sliver of your life in this tale. May your path ever be charmed!

About the Author

> "*Darkling* was inspired by a dream that most would consider a nightmare. I didn't realize I'd written a story about grief until I was done, and I hope that its message will help others as much as the writing helped me."

K.M. Rice is a national award-winning screenwriter and author who has worked for both Magic Leap and Weta Workshop. Her first novel, *Darkling*, now has a companion novel titled *The Watcher*.

Her novella *The Wild Frontier* is an ode to the American spirit of adventure and seeks to awaken the wildish nature in all of us. She also provided additional writing and research for Middle-earth From Script to Screen: Building the World of The Lord of the Rings and The Hobbit. Her upcoming *Afterworld* series is set to debut with the first book, *Ophelia*.

Over the years, her love of storytelling has led to producing and geeking out in various webshows and short films. When not writing or filming, she can be found hiking in the woods, baking, running, and enjoying the company of the many animals on her family ranch in the Santa Cruz Mountains of California.

To find out more and join the wildling community:

www.kmrice.com
kmriceauthor@gmail.com

More by K.M. Rice:

NOVELS

- *The Watcher* (A companion novel to *Darkling*)
- *The Wild Frontier*
- *The Country Beyond the Forests*
- *Afterworld Book I: Ophelia*

AS A CONTRIBUTING AUTHOR

- *Middle-earth From Script to Screen: Building the World of the Lord of the Rings and the Hobbit*
- *Middle-earth Madness*